# Bloody Valentine

## BY MELISSA DE LA CRUZ

Blue Bloods
Masquerade
Revelations
The Van Alen Legacy
Misguided Angel

Keys to the Repository
Bloody Valentine

# Bloody Valentine

## A *Blue Bloods*
### NOVELLA

## Melissa de la Cruz

www.atombooks.net

ATOM

First published in the United States in 2010 by Hyperion
First published in Great Britain in 2010 by Atom

Text and illustrations copyright © 2010 by Melissa de la Cruz
The moral right of the author has been asserted.

A CIP catalogue record for this book
is available from the British Library.

ISBN 978-1-907410-20-8

Printed and bound in Great Britain by
Clays Ltd, St Ives plc

Papers used by Atom are natural, renewable and
recyclable products sourced from well-managed forests and certified
in accordance with the rules of the Forest Stewardship Council.

**Mixed Sources**
Product group from well-managed
forests and other controlled sources
www.fsc.org  Cert no. SGS-COC-004081
© 1996 Forest Stewardship Council

Atom
An imprint of
Little, Brown Book Group
100 Victoria Embankment
London EC4Y 0DY

An Hachette UK Company
www.hachette.co.uk

www.atombooks.net

*For my readers.*
*You guys are the best.*

*Loving, for a long while ahead and far on into life, is solitude, a heightened and deepened kind of aloneness for the person who loves.*

—Rainer Maria Rilke,
"Letters to a Young Poet"

*Love is a battlefield.*

—Pat Benatar

# JUST ANOTHER NIGHT
## IN SUCK CITY*

New York

November

*with apologies to Nick Flynn

## ONE

# *The Holiday Cocktail Lounge*

It was always Christmas down at the Holiday Cocktail Lounge on St. Mark's Place in the East Village; the twinkling lights were left hanging up on the crossbeams year-round, just like the silver tinsel looped around the edge of the counter and the cheerful tree in the back, its ornaments glittering in the dim light. The Holiday, as the regulars called it, was a New York institution. The bar had been a speakeasy during Prohibition, and counted as its patrons the poet W. H. Auden, who lived next door, and Trotsky, who bunked across the street.

No one could put a finger on why the bar had lasted so long. Its resilient popularity was an anomaly in a town where velvet-rope emporiums serving thousand-dollar champagne bottles had become the norm. Maybe it was the custom-made cocktails—the bartender always seemed to know what you wanted to drink—or maybe it was the cozy, quiet feel of the place that murmured a welcome to every weary patron that walked through its doors. Or maybe it was the way the Rolling Stones sounded from the ancient jukebox, all heart and yearning. Time did not just stop at the Holiday, it came to a standstill, frozen in amber as thick and viscous as the home-brewed whiskey it served.

Interestingly enough, not once in its long life had it ever been raided, its swell of underage patrons never rounded up in paddy wagons and hauled off to the local precinct. While its neighbors routinely lost permits and licenses, the Holiday thrived and survived, serving its core clientele: the young and hip, the old and tired, hardened city journalists from the warring tabloids, and droves of tourists looking for an "authentic" New York experience.

It was late November, and in a few weeks the Holiday's year-round frippery would soon be relevant again. During the Christmas season the owners of the establishment liked to add new trimmings—a lush green wreath nailed to the door, colorful hooked rugs featuring

Santa and his elves, an elegant menorah by the window.

When Oliver Hazard-Perry walked in at half past five that afternoon, the place was packed. Oliver had been coming to the bar ever since he procured his first fake ID at fourteen. He turned up his collar and shuffled in, past the regular crew of men with long faces and low voices, who sipped their drinks as slowly as they nursed their failures.

Oliver took the very last seat at the counter, away from the exuberant college kids who'd had an early start and were already fumbling at darts. The Holiday held no attraction for the legions of fresh-faced hedge-funders eager to show off their black American Express cards. (In any event, the Holiday only took cash.) The Holiday was a port in the storm for those seeking shelter, for no matter what happened outside its doors—bankruptcy, apocalypse, collapse—one could find comfort and solace with a drink at its bar.

It was exactly what kept Oliver coming back. Just being at the Holiday made him feel better somehow.

"The usual?" the bartender asked.

Oliver nodded, grateful and a bit flattered to have been recognized. It had never happened before, but then, up until a week ago, he had never visited with much regularity. The bartender slid over a tumbler of the Holiday's famous whiskey. Oliver slammed back the shot, then another and another. Drinking whiskey reminded him of how Schuyler once told him whiskey was the nearest to the taste of his blood. Like salt and fire. His sadness was something he picked at, like the scabs on his neck. He liked to scratch them until they bled, to see how much worse he could make them feel. He really should stop drinking whiskey. It reminded him too much of her. But then, everything in the goddamn city reminded him of her.

There was no escape. At night he dreamed of her, of their year together, of how they would sleep, back to back. He would remember how her hair smelled after a shower, or how her eyes crinkled when she smiled. In the mornings, when he woke up, he was a zombie, listless and anxious. She had left only a month ago, and would not return. Not to him at least; he had seen to that. He had practically given her away, not that she was his to give, but she would never have left otherwise. He understood the extent of her loyalty, as it ran as deep as his own.

He had done the right thing—he knew that—but it hurt nonetheless. It hurt because he knew she loved him;

she had told him as much. It was just—just not *enough*, just not the same way as she loved the other. Oliver did not want to be second best, a consolation prize; he did not desire loyalty and friendship. He wanted her whole heart, and knowing that he would never have it was a difficult cross to bear.

If only he could forget about her. But his very blood yearned for her, for her soft lips to kiss his neck, for the feel of her fangs as they pierced his skin and filled him with an overwhelming wave of contentment. Now his entire body was attuned to its loss. It grieved and mourned along with his soul. He raised a finger for still another pour.

"Easy there, cowboy," the bartender said with smile. "What is that, your fourth already? It's not even six o'clock."

"I need it," Oliver mumbled.

"For what?"

He shook his head, and the bartender moved to take care of her customers on the other side of the counter.

Oliver fingered the card hidden in his pocket, tracing over the engraved words. It was a secret place that served humans like him—Red Bloods who had been abandoned by their vampires, human familiars who were now aching with need. He remembered his brave words to Mimi on the night they first visited the place, the false bravado he'd mustered. It was all a lie. He knew he would end up back there soon enough. He needed a fix, just one bite—it no longer mattered that Schuyler would not be administering it, he just wanted to feel whole again. He wanted someone to make the pain go away. To help him forget. Of course he knew the dangers, the risks—schizophrenia, infection, addiction; the possibility that after one night he might never want to leave. But he had to go. Anything was better than living with the terrible loneliness. He slammed back the shot with a vengeance, pounded the empty glass on the table, and signaled to the bartender again.

"Whatever it is you think you need that for, maybe you shouldn't do it," she said, as she wiped down the counter and gave him a cool once-over. The bartender had been working at the Holiday ever since he had started sneaking in when he was in eighth grade, and Oliver noticed for the first time that she never seemed to age. She looked exactly the same, not a day over eighteen, with long curly hair and intense green eyes. Her tiny white ribbed tanktop showed just a hint of her tanned, flat belly. Oliver had always harbored a little crush on her but had been too shy to do anything about it aside from leaving generous tips. Not that it was hopeless, but it was like being attracted to a movie star—the possibility of having one's affection returned was very low to zero.

To his surprise, she seemed to take an interest. "I'm Freya," she said, holding out a hand.

"Oliver," he said, giving it a firm shake. Her skin was as soft as cashmere. He tried not to blush.

"I know. The kid with the fake ID from Hawaii," she said with a laugh. "Why is it always Hawaii? Is it because it's an easy one to copy? It must be. Oh, don't look too surprised, I've known for years."

"You guys don't get raided?"

"Just let them try." Freya winked. "So. Haven't seen you here in a year or so. Now you're back every night. What's up?"

He shook his head.

"Where's your little friend?" she asked. "You guys always used to come in together."

"She's gone."

"Ah." Freya nodded. "It's her loss."

Oliver laughed hollowly. "Yeah, right." Her loss. He didn't doubt that Schuyler missed him; of course she would. But he knew she was happier now that she was with Jack. The loss was all his. He reached for his wallet and fished out several twenty-dollar bills.

The sexy bartender dismissed them with a wave. "Your money's no good tonight. Just do me a favor. Whatever you're about to do, please don't. Because it's not going to help."

He shook his head and placed a few dollars on the counter as a tip. "Thanks for the drinks, but I have no idea what you're talking about," he mumbled, not meeting her eyes. What did she know about what he was planning? What did she care?

Oliver walked out into the cloudless New York night. It was the kind of evening that not too long ago would have found him and Schuyler traipsing around the city, with only their whims to lead them. There would be no more late-night cappuccinos at Café Reggio. No more sneaking into tiny little pubs to hear the latest folk-singers. No more ending the night and greeting the day with dawn breakfasts at Yaffa. There would be no more of that. Not again. Not ever.

No matter. His car and driver were idling by the curb. He gave the address. After tonight, he would forget everything, including her name. With luck, he would probably forget his own.

# Two

## *Poisoned Apple*

*O*liver had not expected the blood house, which looked like a turn-of-the-century bordello, with velvet couches and dim lighting, to have such a modern medical facility in its quarters. The cigar-chomping madam who sent him to the top floor told him he had to pass a physical before she could register him as a house familiar.

"We need to make sure you don't have any inconvenient diseases for our clients," the doctor explained as he shone a flashlight down Oliver's throat.

Oliver tried to nod, but his mouth was open, so he settled on silence. Afterward, he was poked and prodded with an array of needles that drew his blood. When the physical examination was over, he was brought to another room, where he was introduced to the house psychiatrist.

"De-familiarizing, that is, taking out the markers from your original vampire, is not a physical process," the doctor said. "The poison in your blood is the manifestation of the love you feel for your vampire. What we do here is *eradicate* that love and disavow the hold it has on your psyche, thus eliminating the poison.

"It may be a painful journey, and one whose outcome is unpredictable. Some familiars experience a loss akin to a death. Others lose all their memories of their vampire. Every case is different, as is every relationship between vampire and familiar." The doctor began scribbling on his pad. "Can you tell me a little about your relationship?"

"We were friends," Oliver replied. "I've known her all my life. I was her Conduit." He was relieved that the doctor did not seem to have an adverse reaction to the news. "I loved her. I still love her. Not just because she's my vampire—it's more than that."

"How so?"

"I mean, I loved her before she bit me." He thought of how he'd tried to fool himself, thinking that he'd only loved her once she had transformed. It wasn't true. He had loved her his entire life. He'd only been lying to himself to feel better.

"I see. And the Sacred Kiss. Was it her idea or yours?"

"It was both of ours, I guess. I don't remember really. . . . We were supposed to do it earlier but chickened out and then . . . it just happened. We didn't really plan for it, not then."

"So it was her idea."

"I think so."

The doctor ordered him to close his eyes, and Oliver did so dutifully.

"Let's start at the beginning. Let's remember all the happy memories, then one by one, reject them. Let them go."

The doctor's voice was in his head. It was a compulsion, he realized.

*You are not bound to her.*

*You are no longer hers.*

As the doctor's calm voice droned on, images began to flash in Oliver's mind. Schuyler at five: shy and mute. Schuyler at nine: teasing and petulant. Schuyler at fifteen: beautiful and quiet. The Mercer Hotel. The fumbling and the awkwardness. Then in her childhood bedroom, where it finally happened. The sweet smell of her—of her jasmine and honeysuckle perfume. The sharpness of her fangs as they pierced his skin.

Oliver could feel the wetness on his cheeks. He was crying. It was too much. Schuyler was in every part of his soul, in his blood; she was as necessary to him as his skin. He could not let go.

What was he doing? He didn't belong here. This was against the Code. If the Repository found out, he would be kicked out of service. It would humiliate his family and destroy their reputation. He couldn't remember why he had even come. He began to panic and started looking for a way out, but the litany continued, drumming the compulsion into his head.

*You are no longer her familiar.*

*You are nobody.*

No. No. It's not true. Oliver felt wretched and confused. He did not want to let go of his love for Schuyler. Even if it pained him so much that he could no longer sleep, could no longer eat. He wanted to keep these memories. His sixteenth birthday, when Schuyler had drawn his portrait and bought him an ice-cream cake with two hearts on it. No. He had to hold on. . . . He had to. . . . He had to. . . . He could let go. He could listen to the nice calm voice and let go. Let it all go.

He was no one.

He was nobody.

The nightmare ended.

When he woke up, he found the faces of the doctors peering down at him. A voice—he wasn't sure whose—said, "The lab reports came back. He's clean. Put him in the line."

A few minutes later he was standing in the lobby alongside a group of young familiars. Oliver swayed on his feet. His head hurt, and he couldn't remember what he was doing there or why he had come. But he didn't have time to think or puzzle over his muddled thoughts, because the curtains suddenly parted and a beautiful vampire entered the room.

*"Bonsoir,"* she greeted him. She was model-tall and carried herself with the confidence of a queen. She was from the European Coven, he could tell, with her immaculately tailored traveling clothes and sultry French accent. Her bondmate walked in after her. He was tall and thin with a mop of shaggy dark hair and a

languid expression. They looked like two sleek cats, all angles and black turtlenecks, with their Gauloises cigarettes and sloe-eyed good looks.

"You," she purred, looking directly at Oliver. "Come with me."

Her partner chose a dazed-looking teenage girl, and the two humans followed the couple to one of the elaborate rooms on the top floor. Most of the blood house was furnished as perfunctorily as possible, with thin curtains dividing the rooms. But this was as plush as a five-star hotel suite, a grand space with a sumptuous fur-lined throw on the king-size bed, gilded mirrors, and baroque furnishings.

The male vampire pulled the girl down to the bed, slid her dress off, and immediately began to drink from her. Oliver watched but did not understand. He wasn't sure what he was doing in the room, only that he had been chosen and wanted.

"Wine?" the female vampire asked, holding up a crystal decanter from the glass-topped bar.

"I'm all right, thanks."

"Relax, I won't bite." She laughed. "At least, not yet." She took a long slow sip from her glass and watched her bondmate drain the girl. "That looks delicious."

She put out her cigarette, stubbing it on the Persian rug and leaving a small brown hole.

"My turn," she said, pushing Oliver down on one of the antique armchairs. The vampire straddled him and kissed his neck. She smelled like heavy oily perfume and her skin was papery. She was not as young as she first looked. "This way, please," she said, turning his body toward the front of the room. "He likes to watch."

He saw the male vampire leaning up on his elbow, smiling lasciviously, while the human girl lay unconscious and naked on the bedspread. Oliver did not flinch. He remembered now why he had come to this place.

The vampire had chosen him. Once she sank her fangs into his skin, he would have everything that he wanted. . . . He would experience the Sacred Kiss again. . . . His body needed it. . . . He wanted it so much. . . .

He closed his eyes.

The vampire's breath was hot and smelled like cigarettes; it was like kissing an ashtray, and the pungent smell took him away from the moment.

*"Whatever you're about to do. It's not going to help."*

He blinked and saw a gentle, kind face looking at him. Who was she? Freya, he remembered. She was worried about him. Freya was so beautiful, more beautiful than the vampire in his lap, whose looks were mere glamour, a sad façade hiding a wretched interior. Freya glowed with an incandescent light. She had a spark in her eyes. She had told him not to do this.

What was he doing?

Why was he here?

Then he remembered . . . the blood house. Wait. What had he done? He could live with the sorrow of losing her. He could live with missing . . . who was he missing? He couldn't remember . . . but then with a jolt all his memories came flooding back. It was as if he were waking up. He felt alive again. He could live with the pain. But he would never forgive himself for doing this. He could not forget. He would not. He would never forget . . . Schuyler . . .

Schuyler.

Freya.

Schuyler.

The vampire bit his neck and fell back, screaming, her face scarred by the acid in his blood. "Poison! Poison! He is still marked!"

Oliver ran out of the room as fast as he could.

## THREE

### *Cleaning Up*

*I*t was close to four in the morning when he returned to the Holiday. Freya was standing behind the bar, hitting the side of a cocktail glass with a knife. "Last call. Last call, everyone." When she saw Oliver, she smiled. "You're back." She studied his face. "You didn't do it."

"No. I . . . almost did." He did not wonder anymore how she knew where he had been or what he had been about to do. "I didn't because I was thinking of you."

"Good boy." She smiled as she pointed toward the utility closet. "Come on, help me clean up. A little elbow grease will make you feel better. Then I'll let you walk me home."

Oliver took a broom and began to sweep the floor and pick up the plastic straws and soggy napkins that had fallen there. He helped wipe down the counter and dry the glasses. He stacked them neatly on the back shelves. Freya was right: the physical labor made him feel better.

The last of the regulars stumbled out, and the two of them were left alone. He looked around, realizing that over the years he had never seen anyone work here but Freya. How did one tiny girl keep the whole place together?

When the bar was tidied and clean, Freya shrugged on a green army flak jacket, oversized and gigantic on her small frame. It was the kind of jacket worn by Special Forces teams parachuting into jungles, and it looked incongruous against her delicate features, which made the whole effect even more charming. She pulled up the hood to cover her hair. "Come on, I'm just down the street."

On the way to her apartment, Freya stopped by the Korean grocer on the corner. She chose a bouquet of flowers, two tubs of fresh fruit, and a spray of mint. Unlike the usual lackluster offerings found at the corner deli, everything Freya touched seemed to glow: the strawberries red and succulent, the melons shone with orange intensity. The mint smelled like it had just been picked from a field in Provence.

She led him to a shabby tenement building with a broken front door. "We didn't get the gentrification memo," she joked. He followed her up the stairs to the third landing. It had four doors, and she opened the one painted red. "Thank goodness I face out to the street. Those two over there just look at the courtyard."

It was a small apartment by anyone's standards, but in terms of New York real estate, even tinier still. There was an old-fashioned claw-foot tub in the middle of the room and a minuscule galley kitchen with aging appliances. Against the window was a four-poster bed draped with a paisley print tapestry. But once Oliver entered the room, he was startled to find it was not as small as it had looked from the doorway. He had been mistaken. The apartment was large and magnificent, with a library full of books on one side and a proper formal dining room on the other.

"Sit," she said, pointing to a grand settee that he was certain had not been there before.

There were ancestral portraits on the wall, and what looked like museum-quality art. Was that a Van

Dyck? That one was surely a Rembrandt. The usual bohemian squalor had vanished, and instead Oliver was sitting on a proper couch in an elegantly furnished living room with a cracking fireplace. The windows to the fire escape still looked out onto Avenue C, but Oliver could swear he heard the ocean.

Freya disappeared into the back bedroom to change (again, he hadn't seen it from the doorway—and what happened to the four-poster bed? And the claw-foot tub? Was he losing his mind?). When she returned she was wearing flannel pajamas. She fired up the stove— a sleek industrial design and not the old and ugly white one he had seen from the doorway—and began to crack eggs. "You need breakfast," she murmured as she chopped the mint.

A delicious buttery smell began to waft from the kitchen, and after a few minutes, Freya placed two plates on the table in the little breakfast nook. By this time, Oliver had accepted the fact that the apartment was not quite what it was, and he was no longer surprised by the appearance of yet another cozy and beautiful piece of furniture. Was this a dream? If so, he wanted to keep sleeping.

Oliver took a bite. The eggs were soft and creamy,

and the mint gave them a sharp and interesting taste. He finished the whole thing in three bites.

"You were hungry," Freya observed, pulling up her knees to her chin.

He nodded and wiped his hands with a linen napkin. He watched as she ate her eggs slowly, savoring every bite. "Tell me about her," Freya said, licking her fork.

"She was my best friend." He told her everything about his friendship with Schuyler from the beginning to the bittersweet end. He found that with Freya, he could talk about Schuyler without feeling pain. He laughed and reveled in the memories. Oliver talked into the late morning hours. He dimly remembered helping with the dishes, and then falling asleep in her bed.

"You are too young to be so lost and so bereaved," Freya had whispered, before he closed his eyes.

When he woke up later that afternoon, he had his arms around her.

## FOUR

*Under New Ownership*

liver went back to school and to his life. He felt better than he had in weeks, and he was looking forward to seeing Freya again. She had been hard to reach, neither picking up her phone nor returning his calls, but school and Repository work had kept him busy. It wasn't until a week later that he returned to the Holiday Cocktail Lounge.

He noticed there was something different about the place as soon as he arrived. For one, there was a bouncer at the door with a flashlight who glared at his fake ID.

"Hawaii, huh?" the big gorilla asked skeptically.

"Look, I don't want a drink. I'm just here to see Freya."

"No one here by that name."

"C'mon, man."

"You can ask Mack, but he won't tell you different," the bouncer said, handing him back his ID. "But order a drink and you're out of here."

Oliver nodded his thanks and entered the bar. The bouncer wasn't the only thing new. There were three bartenders behind the counter now. Two old men wearing bow ties, and a pretty girl who had the steely beauty of an aspiring actress but none of Freya's charm. Even the crowd was different—polished and sleek in designer duds as they tilted back pastel-colored drinks in martini glasses. There was a leather-bound menu with brand-name spirits.

It was a sea of strangers. Where were the arguing tabloid journalists, the old men with long faces, the young kids at the dartboard? Speaking of, where was the dartboard? And the pool table? Sure, the Christmas lights were still up, but now there was a mechanical singing Santa, and instead of being infused with an offbeat, nostalgic charm akin to a well-worn watering hole, the Holiday looked like a plastic replica of what it had been.

Oliver shook his head and fought his way to a fancy

bar stool. He ordered a sparkling water and waited. Even if the Holiday had changed, Freya was always here. She had to be.

Hours passed. Customers left. The bartenders glared at him. But Oliver sat there until last call.

# FIVE

## *Love and Courage*

Oliver did not know how long he waited, standing on the sidewalk with a bouquet of lilies, but around four in the morning, she finally arrived. She was still wearing the puffy flak jacket from the other night, but this time she had kept the hood down, and her curly hair danced in the breeze.

"What are you doing here?" she asked, and Oliver was relieved to notice she did not sound angry, only mildly amused. "Hold this," she said, handing him her grocery bag as she removed her keys from her purse.

"I waited for you at the Holiday. You never showed," he said. "Did I do something wrong? Do you not want to see me?"

Freya shook her head and unlocked the main door. They walked up the narrow staircase. "How did you find me?" she asked, as she led the way into her apartment.

Oliver crinkled his brow. It had been difficult. He had been sure she lived on Seventh Street and Avenue C. But he had walked the entire block and not come across the Korean deli or the shabby tenement building with the red awning. He had all but given up when he realized it was right in front of him. How had he not noticed before?

"I don't know, really." Oliver settled into one of the cozy chairs. "What happened to the Holiday? It's different. You're not there."

"I sold it. I'm moving."

"Why?"

"It was time," she said. She crossed her arms. "You look better."

"Thanks to you," he said.

"Tea?" she asked.

"Sure." He waited while she boiled water and fixed him a cup. When she placed the teacup in front of him, he took her hand and held it for a long while. He wanted her so much. She looked down at him. For a moment they stood without speaking.

"I thought I had done everything I needed to do," she finally said.

"Why are you keeping me away? I'm not a boy." He pulled her closer and she sat on his lap.

She ruffled his hair. "No, you're not. You're right."

He leaned over and kissed her. He had never kissed a girl other than Schuyler. But this time, he wasn't thinking at all of Schuyler, only of Freya.

Freya smelled like milk and honey and the wonderful scent of spring. He felt her move against him, and he pulled her closer so that he could put his hand on her chest. He felt his heart begin to pound—he was so nervous—what was he doing—he did not know how to do this—had not planned for this—and yet . . . he heard Freya sigh, but it was not a sigh of exasperation . . . it was the sound of acceptance and invitation.

"Come with me," she said, and led him to the bed.

She undressed and slipped underneath the covers. She looked as beautiful as a Botticelli painting. Oliver's hands trembled as he quickly removed his clothing and joined her under the blankets. He was so nervous—what if she laughed? What if he did it wrong somehow? Could one get it wrong? He wasn't so innocent, but he wasn't so experienced either. What if she didn't like what he. . . . Her body was warm and inviting, and he fell on her like a thirsty man in front of a waterfall. He stopped doubting. Stopped worrying. Stopped feeling nervous.

It was his first time. With Schuyler, they had been waiting for the right time, or perhaps they had waited because they knew the right time would never arrive. It didn't matter. Only Freya mattered now.

Her hands felt warm and light on his body, and he shivered against her. Her soft mouth on his neck kissed him sweetly. She pulled him ever closer, and then they were joined together. Her body rippled underneath him, and he looked into her eyes and heard her cry out for him.

There was so much to feel, so much to see. He was in and outside of his body, in and outside of his blood. He was flying above the ceiling, looking at the two of them from below, marveling at how sleek and slippery their limbs were as they rolled together, the beautiful shape they made, their bodies intertwined. It felt as if she were turning him inside out, and all he could do was keep doing what he was doing, and he felt her all around and inside his body and inside his soul.

When it was over, he was covered in sweat and

shaking. He opened his eyes and saw he was still in the same room, looking at the same cracked ceiling. "I love you," he said, over and over again. "I love you, Freya."

Freya looked at him tenderly. "No, you don't, my darling. But you are no longer in pain."

## SIX

## *A Last Good-bye*

The next morning they had breakfast at Veselka, a Ukrainian diner that was famous for its borscht. Oliver felt ravenous and energized. He did not know if it was the loss of sleep or the love they had made, but he felt like a new man. He felt sufficiently brave enough to ask Freya the question he had been dreading the moment he noticed the Holiday had been irrevocably changed.

"Where are you going?" he asked, spearing a pierogi and covering it with sour cream.

"My family is moving back home. To North Hampton."

"Why?"

"It's complicated," she said ruefully. "A story for another day."

Oliver settled against the booth, feeling the cracked leather dig into his skin. Did he feel better? Different? Worse? Better. Definitely better. He touched the side of his neck. He did not feel the same throb there.

Schuyler. He could say her name. He could remember her without the pain. Remember and honor their love, their friendship, but no longer be tortured by her absence. It was as if Schuyler was behind glass. Part of his past but no longer the torment of his future. He missed his friend. But he would survive her loss. *Her* loss.

He put down his fork. "Who are you? What are you?" he asked Freya.

"I'm a witch." She smiled. "But then I think you already knew that, scribe."

"You know about the Blue Bloods?"

"Yes. Of course. We have to. But we keep away from their business. My family does not like to . . . intervene. But you were a special case."

"Will I ever see you again?"

"Maybe," Freya said thoughtfully. "But I don't think you'll need to."

She was right. He did not love her. He had loved her last night, as it was love that they had shared together. And now she was going away, but it was all right.

Oliver was himself again. He had the memories of his time as Schuyler's human familiar, but he no longer felt the ache of need, the suffering in his very soul. Whatever he had felt for Schuyler had not been removed forcibly. Instead, his love had been absorbed and dispersed into his spirit. It would always be a part of him, but it did not have the power to hurt him anymore. Freya had done this. She had healed him. Freya, the witch.

"Thank you." He rose to kiss her on the forehead. "Thank you so much."

"Oh, sweetheart, it was my pleasure."

One last hug, and then they parted.

Oliver walked down the street in the opposite direction. His cell phone began to vibrate, and when he saw the number, he answered it immediately. He listened for a moment, and his face broke into a smile. "Really? Wow. Congratulations. When? Of course I'll be there. I wouldn't miss it for the world."

# Freya Beauchamp's Scrambled Eggs for the Brokenhearted*

*(For those who like their breakfasts fortified by a little magic)*

| | |
|---|---|
| **eggs** | **salt** |
| **heavy cream** | **black pepper** |
| **chopped fresh mint** | **butter** |

As you chop the mint, repeat these lines:

> *Broken hearts take a toll.*
> *Mint shall heal the shattered soul.*
> *The Goddess breathes new life in you.*
> *Go forth and find a love that's true.*

Whisk the eggs with the cream in a bowl. Add the chopped mint, salt, and pepper. Melt the butter on a pan over medium heat. Add the egg mixture; cook two minutes without stirring. Using a large spoon, gently turn over until it is cooked through but still soft.

Garnish with mint sprigs.

Serves one broken heart and one friendly one.

—Adapted from *The Book of White Magic* by Ingrid Beauchamp

*For more about Freya and her spellcipes, watch out for *Witches of East End*, due Summer 2011 from Hyperion.

# Always Something There to Remind Me

Endicott Academy

Endicott, Massachusetts, 1985

# ONE

## *Patient Zero*

When Allegra Van Alen woke up, her head hurt and it took her a moment to recognize her surroundings. She was wearing a hospital gown, but she knew she was still at Endicott, since the view outside her room showed the white clapboard chapel in the distance. She must be in the student clinic then, which was confirmed by the appearance of the school nurse holding a tray of cookies.

Mrs. Anderson was a universally beloved caregiver who watched over the students with a motherly eye and always made sure there was fresh fruit in the refectory. She walked in with a concerned smile. "How are you feeling, dear?"

"I guess I'll survive," Allegra said ruefully. "What happened?"

"Accident on the field. They said you got hit by the ball."

"Ouch." She grimaced, scratching the bandage around her forehead.

"You're lucky; doctor said it would have taken out a Red Blood."

"How long was I out?"

"Just a few hours."

"Any chance I can get out of here today? I have a Latin test tomorrow, and I have to study." Allegra groaned. Like the rest of the school, the clinic was comfortable enough. It was housed in a cozy New England cottage, with white wicker furniture and bright floral curtains. But right then she wanted nothing more than to be in the refuge of her own room, with its black-and-white Cure posters, old-fashioned rolltop secretary desk, and newly purchased Walkman, so she could be alone and listen to Depeche Mode. Even in the clinic, she could hear strains of a Bob Dylan song wafting from the open windows. Everyone else at school listened to the same music from twenty years ago, as if prep-school life was stuck in a sixties time warp. Allegra had nothing against

Dylan, but she didn't see the need for all the angst.

Mrs. Anderson shook her head as she fluffed Allegra's pillows and set her patient back against the feathery plumpness. "Not just yet. Dr. Perry's coming in from New York to check on you in a bit. Your mother insisted."

Allegra sighed. Of course Cordelia would insist. Her mother watched over her like a hawk, with more than the usual maternal concern. Cordelia approached motherhood as if it were akin to guarding a precious Ming vase. She treated her daughter with kid gloves, and always acted as if Allegra was one nervous breakdown away from being sent to the nuthouse, even though anyone could see that Allegra was the very picture of health. She was popular, cheerful, athletic, and spirited.

Life under Cordelia's care was suffocating, to say the least. It was why Allegra could not wait until she turned eighteen and got out of the house for good. Her mother's all-consuming anxiety over her well-being was one of the reasons she had campaigned to transfer out of Duchesne and enroll at Endicott. In New York, Cordelia's influence was inescapable. More than anything, Allegra just wanted to be free.

Mrs. Anderson finished taking her temperature and put away the thermometer. "You have a few visitors waiting outside. Shall I send them in?"

"Sure." Allegra nodded. Her head was starting to feel a little better—either from the melted chocolate in Mrs. Anderson's famous cookies or from the massive painkillers, she wasn't sure.

"All right, team, you can come in. But don't tire her. I can't have her relapse now. Gentle, gentle." With a last smile, the friendly nurse left the room. In a moment, Allegra's hospital bed was surrounded by the entire girls' field hockey team. They crowded around, breathless and windswept, still wearing their uniforms: green plaid kilts, white polo shirts, and green knee-high socks.

"Oh my god!" "Are you okay?" "Dude, that thing careened off your head!" "We're gonna get that bitch from Northfield Mount Hermon next time!" "Don't worry, they got flagged!" "Oh my god, you totally blacked out! We were sure we couldn't see you till tomorrow!"

The cheerful cacophony filled the room, and Allegra grinned. "It's all right. I got free cookies; you guys want some?" she asked, pointing to the platter by the windowsill. The girls fell on the cookies like a hungry mob.

"Wait—you guys haven't told me! Did we win?" Allegra asked.

"What do you think? We kicked ass, Captain." Birdie Belmont, Allegra's best friend and roommate, gave her a mock salute that would have been more impressive if she hadn't been holding a giant chocolate chip cookie in her right hand.

The girls gossiped conspiratorially when a male voice interrupted from the other side of the curtain that divided the room in two. "Hey, you guys have cookies over there? Aren't you going to share?"

The team giggled. "Your neighbor," Birdie whispered. "I think he's hungry."

"Excuse me?" Allegra called. She hadn't even noticed that she was sharing a room until now. Maybe she *had* suffered a pretty hard blow to the head and not just a run-of-the-mill field injury.

Rory Antonini, a talented midfielder with the best scoring percentage in the league, pulled back the curtain that separated the room. "Hey, Bendix," the girls chorused.

Bendix Chase was the most popular boy in their

class. It wasn't hard to figure out why: at six feet three, he looked a bit like a young blond giant, with his broad shoulders and powerful build. His face resembled that of a Greek god's: with a fine brow, a perfect nose, and cut-glass cheekbones. He had a dimple on each cheek, and his clear, cornflower-blue eyes twinkled with fun. He was lying on a hospital bed with his right leg in a cast. He waved cheerfully.

"When are you getting out?" asked Darcy Sedrik, their goaltender, as she handed him the almost empty plate of cookies.

"Today. Cast is finally coming off. Thank god— I'm tired of hopping to class," Bendix said, nodding his gratitude for the cookie. "What happened to you?" he asked Allegra.

"Merely a flesh wound," she said, pointing to her gauze turban and affecting a British accent.

"At least you still have your arms," Bendix mused with a smile at the Monty Python quote.

Allegra tried not to seem overly charmed that he had picked up the reference so quickly.

She didn't want to appear as just another of his googly-eyed fan club, as the entire field hockey team had now migrated over to his side of the room to sign his cast with heart-shaped dots over their i's and innumerable X's and O's.

"Visiting hours are over, I'm afraid," Mrs. Anderson declared, reappearing in her starched white uniform. There was another chorus of "Aww" as she shooed the girls out. She was about to close the curtain that separated her two patients when Bendix asked if they could keep it open.

"I hope you don't mind. It gets a bit claustrophobic. And your side has the TV," he said.

"Sure." Allegra shrugged. She and Bendix knew each other, of course, as Stuart Endicott Academy, like the Duchesne School, was a small and tight-knit community of the breathtakingly advantaged children of the elite. However, unlike the rest of the female population, she did not swoon in his presence. She found his all-American good looks a bit too obvious, too Hollywood movie star, too universally admired. Bendix looked like the jock from *The Breakfast Club*, except even more handsome. And Bendix wasn't just good looking and athletic and adored, he was also, shockingly, for a boy of his privilege and status—kind. Allegra noticed that far from being an arrogant snob who stalked the halls with his massive ego, Bendix was genuinely nice to everyone, even her brother Charles, which was saying something.

Still, even if the most gorgeous boy at Endicott was sitting mere feet away, watching music videos with her (why on earth was Eddie Murphy singing? And what was up with that striped shirt he was wearing?), Allegra paid him no more thought.

# TWO

## *The Van Alen Twins*

When Dr. Perry arrived from New York, he pronounced Allegra well as ever, and she was back in her dormitory the next day. She was running between classes when she saw her brother walking purposefully across the quadrangle toward her.

"I came as soon as I heard," Charles Van Alen said, taking her elbow gently. "Who did it? Are you sure you're all right? Cordelia is beside herself. . . ."

Allegra rolled her eyes. Her twin brother was such a dork sometimes. Not only because he insisted on calling their mother by her first name, but also because of his whole big-protector act. Especially since she was taller than him by two inches. "I'm fine, Charlie, really." She knew he hated being called by his childhood nickname, but she couldn't help it. He was the last person she wanted to see right then.

Unlike Allegra, Charles Van Alen was short for his age. The twins could not have looked less alike, as he had dark hair and cold gray eyes. Unlike his casually dressed peers, Charles wore an ascot to class and carried a leather briefcase. He wasn't very popular at Endicott, not because of his pretensions (although they were many) but mainly because he complained about the school constantly and let everyone know he wouldn't be there if his sister hadn't insisted they transfer. Most of the students thought he was an annoying, pompous windbag, and in return he acted as though they were all beneath him.

Allegra understood that most of his insecurity came from his small stature. If only he would relax—the doctors had agreed he had yet to hit his growth spurt, and there was no question he would be handsome. His face was just a little *off* right now. In a few years he would grow into his nose, and his features—those intense eyes, that deep forehead—would settle into regal symmetry. But for now, Charlie Van Alen was just another nerdy short guy on the debate team.

He had been in Washington, D.C., for the Elocution Finals over the weekend, for which Allegra was glad. Otherwise she knew he would have made a huge fuss at the clinic, and would have probably insisted they transfer her to a better care facility at Mass General or something. Charlie was as bad as Cordelia when it came to looking after Allegra. Between the two of them, she felt like a Dresden doll: precious, fragile, and unable to help herself. It drove her insane.

"Here, let me . . ." he said, taking her bag.

"I can carry my backpack. Let go. Don't be weird," she snapped. She tried not to feel guilty about the shocked, sad look that appeared on his face.

This wasn't any way to speak to her bondmate, but she couldn't help it. Because Charlie was Michael, of course. After what had happened in Florence, there was no question about it now—they had been born as twins in every cycle since then. The House of Records insisted on the practice, so that what had happened back then would never happen again. So that from the beginning, there would be no doubts, no questions, no more mistakes.

Still, every incarnation since had been worse than the last. Allegra couldn't put a finger on it, but over the years she had begun to feel a distance from him. Not only because of what had happened back then— Oh, who was she kidding—it had *everything* to do with what had happened in Florence. She could never forgive herself. Never. It was all her fault. And the fact that he still loved her—would always love her—*forever and ever and ever*—through all the years and the centuries— made her feel more resentful than grateful. His love was a burden. After what had come between them, in every cycle she came closer to believing she did not deserve his love, and with the resentment came the guilt and the anger. She didn't know why, but it had become harder and harder to feel for him what he still felt for her.

It was ironic, really. *She* had been in the wrong, and yet he was the one being punished. It was depressing to think about, and on that bright fall afternoon, she felt as far away from him as she ever had.

"No—let me," he insisted, pulling on the strap.

"Charlie, please!" she yelled, and yanked with all her strength so that her backpack flew out of his hands, and he slipped and fell on the grass.

He glowered at her as he picked himself up and dusted off his pants. "What is wrong with you?" he hissed.

"Just—leave me alone, can't you?" She raised her hands and raked through her long blond hair in frustration.

"But I—I . . ."

*I KNOW. You love me. You've always loved me. You'll ALWAYS love me. I know, Michael. I can hear you loud and clear.*

"Gabrielle!"

"My name is Allegra!" she almost screamed. Why did he have to call her by *that* name all the time? Why did he have to act like people didn't notice how obsessed he was with her? Sure, none of the Blue Bloods kids thought it was weird, since they knew who they were even if they still hadn't had their coming-out yet; but the Red Bloods didn't know their history or what they meant to each other, and it bothered her. This wasn't ancient Egypt anymore; this was the twentieth century. Times had changed. And yet the Conclave was always so slow to react.

Sometimes Allegra just wanted to experience life as it happened, without the burden of her entire immortal history on her shoulders—she was only sixteen years old—at least, in this lifetime. Give her a break. In 1985, in Endicott, Massachusetts, your twin brother's having a crush on you was simply gross and disgusting; and Allegra was beginning to agree with the Red Bloods.

"This guy bothering you, Legs?" Bendix Chase asked, happening upon them as the third bell rang.

"Did this guy just call you 'Legs'?" Charles gaped.

"It's all right," Allegra said, sighing. "Bendix Chase, I don't think you know my brother, Charlie."

"Freshman?" Bendix asked, pumping Charles's hand. "Good to meet you."

"No. We're twins," Charles replied icily. "And I'm in your Shakespeare seminar."

"Sure you guys are related?" Bendix winked. "I don't see the resemblance."

Charles turned red. "Of course we're sure. Now, if you'd excuse us," he said, turning away and pulling Allegra toward him.

"Hey, hey—there's no need to be rude," Bendix said mildly. "You dropped your book." He handed Charles back a textbook that had slipped from his hold when he'd fallen to the ground. Charles neglected to thank him.

"There really isn't, Charlie," Allegra agreed. She moved away from him to stand next to Bendix, who swung an arm around her shoulders.

"I believe we have a Latin midterm today, my dear," Bendix said. "Shall we?"

Allegra allowed the popular jock to lead her away. She would never have done so except that Charles had been so irritating. Served him right. She left her twin, who continued to stare at them, alone in the quadrangle.

## THREE

## *The Only Subject Vampires Aren't Good At*

llegra was a top-notch student, but she was horrible at Latin. She found it difficult to differentiate the bastard Red Blood rendition of the Sacred Language from the real thing, and was constantly messing up. Latin had declensions and three genders, which just didn't make sense to her. She could never keep the real language of the immortals straight from its human, quotidian version.

She stared at the angry red *D−* circled on the top of her test paper. That sucked. If she didn't keep up her grades, Cordelia would pull her out of Endicott and put her back in Duchesne. She would be right where she started: a virtual prisoner of her mother's grand expectations for her future and her future contributions to their race. Seriously, Cordelia spoke like a World War II demagogue sometimes. Not that Allegra had been in cycle then, but she read the Repository reports.

"Phew, that's ugly," Bendix remarked, upon stealing a look at her paper.

"What'd you get?" she asked, arching an eyebrow.

He waved his *A+* in her direction with a smug smile.

Ugh. Why did he have to be so annoyingly perfect? There was nothing Allegra despised more than the word "perfect," other than the people who personified it. She *hated* when people called her perfect, when they couldn't see past her looks, past the waves of lustrous blond hair and the sun-kissed tan and the body. Why anyone could make such a big deal of such superficial things, she would never understand. She thought everyone was beautiful—and not just in some ridiculously saintly way wherein she believed everyone had a beautiful soul. No. Allegra truly believed most of the people she met were beautiful to look at—who cared about a few pounds here or there, or a crooked nose or a weird mole? She loved looking at people. She thought they were gorgeous.

She was just as bad as Bendix when it came down to it, wasn't she? She was perfect to look at, and on top of that, she liked everybody. Sometimes she was so tired of being herself.

"I can help you with Latin, if you'd like," Bendix offered as they gathered their things and began to make their way out of the classroom.

"You're offering to tutor me?" That was new. A Red Blood offering to teach an immortal vampire new tricks. Charlie would sneer. Allegra shook her head. "I think I'll be okay, thanks. Just have to bone up on my nouns."

"Up to you. But you might not be aware, since you just transferred here, that if you don't keep up a decent average you can kiss the field hockey team—and the division championships—good-bye," Bendix said, holding the door open for her.

The man had a point.

Over the next few weeks, Allegra met Bendix at the main library for Latin lessons every other night. What started out as a sincere effort between the two of them to help Allegra learn the language, slowly turned into long and far-reaching discussions about anything and everything: the quality of the food served in the refectory (atrocious), their thoughts on the Palestinian crisis, whether "Abracadabra" by the Steve Miller Band was the worst or best song ever written (Bendix was for best, Allegra voted worst).

One evening, Bendix leaned over the Latin text-book and sighed. His blond bangs fell in his eyes, and Allegra stifled a desire to reach over and push them off his forehead. "Your folks coming up for Parents' Day next week?" he asked. "You're from New York, right?"

Allegra nodded and shook her head at the same time. "Mother is coming, of course. She'd never miss it. My dad . . . is away." That seemed the easiest way to explain Lawrence's absence. "You?"

"Nah. My mom has this board meeting, so she has to stay in San Francisco. Dad can't be bothered. Wouldn't want to interrupt his art."

"Your dad's an artist?"

"He makes found sculptures. So far he hasn't sold one, probably because they look like trash. But don't tell him that."

"It doesn't sound like you like either of them very much," Allegra said, feeling sympathetic. She was very fond of both Lawrence and Cordelia. It was just that she hadn't seen Lawrence in years, and Cordelia had morphed into a shrill, nervous old lady.

"That's the thing of it. I do like my parents quite a

bit, but they've never had a lot of time for me. Oops, did I say that? I hate when I get self-pitying."

Allegra smiled. She opened her Latin textbook. "If you want, I'll share Cordelia with you. She just loves meeting my friends. But I can't speak for Charlie."

"What does your brother have against me, by the way? I never did anything to the guy," he said, looking concerned.

"Oh . . . he'll . . . get over it," Allegra said. She coughed. "Anyway . . . back to Latin?"

"So, are you guys dating or what?" Birdie asked, when Allegra came home to their shared bedroom that evening shortly after midnight.

"Dating? Who? What are you talking about?" Allegra asked, blushing slightly as she put her books away. They never did get to declensions. Instead they had spent the evening talking about the merits of growing up in San Francisco versus New York. Allegra, a lifelong Manhattanite, had argued that "the city" was infinitely superior in every way—in cultural offerings, museums, restaurants—while Bendix defended the city by the bay for its foggy weather, inherent beauty, and liberal politics. Neither of them had been able to convince the other.

"You mean me and Ben?" she asked Birdie. "You think we're a couple?"

"Oh, it's 'Ben' now. Soon you'll be calling him Benny," her friend teased, rolling an herbal cigarette. It was the latest fashion. Allegra didn't mind, except that it stank up the room, and Birdie tended to spray too much air freshener to cover it up during inspection. As a result, their room always smelled like a toilet.

Allegra grimaced. "Ew. Not a chance. We're *friends*."

Her roommate blew a huge smoke ring. "Please, everyone sees how you guys act around each other."

"What? Are you kidding me?"

"Besides, you guys look ridiculously *perfect* together," Birdie said with a grin. She had heard Allegra's rants against the "p-word."

"Good lord!" Allegra shuddered. She just did not see Ben in that way. She liked having someone to talk to, and enjoyed his company. Besides, they could never be together—she could never have feelings for him, not in that way. Birdie was a Red Blood; she didn't know what she was talking about.

"Seriously? Worse things could happen than to date him. His family just sold their company for like, two billion dollars. Did you see the paper today?" Birdie asked, throwing the *Wall Street Journal* toward Allegra.

Allegra read the front-page announcement detailing Allied Corporation's acquisition of the family-run Bendix group of companies and marveled at Ben's modesty. His mother had a "business meeting," which was why she couldn't make it to Parents' Day. More like a major shareholders' conference.

"They are seriously loaded. No wonder he was named after his mom's side of the family. They have all the dough."

"Birdie, don't be crass," Allegra chided. Even at Endicott, it was considered bad form to be too aware of each other's provenance. But after reading the news, she could not help but like Ben even more. Not because she found out he was wealthy—she never cared too much about money, even though she had never lived without it—but because, given the extreme affluence of his background, he was humble and down-to-earth.

And she had gotten the feeling, after talking to him that evening, that Bendix Chase wouldn't have minded having a little less of the stuff people cared too much about, if it meant he could have just a little more of the things that really mattered.

## FOUR

## The Society of Poets and Adventurers

*L*ater that week, Allegra was already asleep when she heard a noise outside her window. She blinked, confused. It was a light, clattering sound. Pebbles. Followed by the sound of giggles. She walked toward the window and opened it. "What's going on?" she asked, slightly annoyed.

A group of hooded strangers stood underneath her window. In an ominous voice, the tallest one intoned darkly, "Allegra Van Alen, your future awaits you."

Oh, right. She had forgotten, although Birdie had warned her the other week. It was Tap Night. The night that Endicott's most prestigious secret society, the Peithologians, inducted its new members. She noticed her roommate's bed was empty, which meant Birdie was already participating in the night's festivities since she was of course a member.

Allegra called, "I'll be right down," just as another group of hooded students entered her room and put a hood over her head. She was now officially kidnapped.

When her hood was removed, Allegra noticed she was in a clearing in the woods. There was a bonfire raging, and she was kneeling with a group of new initiates.

The hooded leader offered her a golden chalice, filled with a reddish libation. "Drink from the cup of knowledge," he directed. Their fingers brushed as he handed her the goblet, and Allegra tried not to giggle as she took a sip. Vodka and 7-Up. Not bad.

"You look silly in that robe," she whispered, for she had recognized his voice the moment he had called her from her window.

"Shhh!" Bendix replied, trying not to laugh as well.

She passed the goblet to the person next to her, wondering who else had been chosen. When all the new members had drunk from the cup, Bendix raised a toast with the glass. "They have consumed the fire of Enlightenment! Welcome to the Peithologians, new Poets and Adventurers! Let us now dance in the woods like the nymphs of Bacchus!" Somewhere in the back, someone banged a gong, and it echoed through the forest.

"The nymphs of Bacchus?" she asked skeptically.

"It's a Greek thing. . . ." He shrugged. The members had removed their hoods, although most were still wearing their robes. More plastic goblets filled with vodka and 7-Up were passed around the group.

"Is this what happens when you become a Peithologian?" Allegra asked, looking around at the merry, drunken crew. "You cut curfew and dance around a fire?"

"Don't forget the cheap cocktails. Very important," Bendix said, nodding.

"This is it? This is what all the fuss is about?" She laughed. The Peithologians had a stellar, jealously guarded reputation at school.

"Pretty much. Oh, and every quarter we have a formal. One is clothing-optional, of course."

"Of course."

"And later we'll have the annual Bad Poetry Contest."

"So it's mostly just . . . silliness?" Allegra asked, although she already knew the answer.

"Why? What do you guys do that's so important in that Committee of yours?"

He knew she was in the Committee. Of course they had one at Endicott, since the school had a sizable group of Blue Blood students. She looked around at the new recruits and felt disappointed not to find her brother among the flushed faces. She knew Charlie would never have been picked, but she felt bad all the same. The Peithologians were one of the reasons her twin hated the school so much. At Endicott, no one thought much of the Committee. Everyone wanted to be part of the Peithologians.

"We do the same things. . . ." Allegra shrugged.

"Yeah, I thought so. Someone should really bring back some old-school stuff. You know. Coffins. Murder. The peddling of influence." He wagged his eyebrows and took a big sip from his oversized goblet. "Oh, here comes Texas. Forsyth. A word! Excuse me," he told her. Bendix walked over to speak to Forsyth Llewellyn, who served as faculty adviser to the society.

Allegra raised her glass to Forsyth, who gave her a courtly nod of his head. He taught freshman English, and she'd seen him around campus. She remembered him, of course. She would never forget those who had been in cycle in Florence.

The party went on for a good hour or so until Bendix raised his voice. "Excuse me, excuse me, ahem."

The crowd quieted, and he waited until he had their full attention. "It is time now to pay tribute and say the words of our founder."

The veteran society members raised their glasses to the sky and, as one, recited the following poem: "'The Bird.' By Killington Jones. *'I think that I have never heard/ A song as lovely as a bird's/With feathers light and beak bright red/The nests he builds to lay his head/Only the Lord can make a bird/But even I can write a turd.'*"

"Right!" Bendix beamed. "Let the Bad Poetry Contest begin!"

Allegra listened, bemused, as a succession of wannabe poets recited a slew of truly terrible verse to the hooting crowd. Bendix brought the house down with his entry, "The Last Song of the Ice Fisherman on the Floes of Dear Old Norway." It was tragically, comically awful, and he won first place.

When it was over, he walked over to her side.

"Congratulations. You're funny," she said, poking him in the chest.

He caught her hand, and held her gaze.

"Ben—stop." She smiled. "Let go," she said, even though she liked the feel of his strong hand around hers. She liked Ben—and it was Ben now—Bendix was so serious and unlike his goofy character—and she didn't mind that he called her Legs—she liked it. It was unserious. It was unlike her. He saw a side of her that no one had really seen yet. To the Blue Bloods, she would always be Gabrielle, the Virtuous, the Responsible, their Queen, their Mother, their Savior. But to Bendix Chase, she was not even Allegra Van Alen, she was Legs. It made her feel young, dangerous, and reckless. Qualities that did not apply to Gabrielle.

Plus, he was so very, very cute.

"Come here," she whispered, pulling him close, tugging on that silly costume robe he was wearing.

"Huh?"

She pulled him closer, and when he saw what she wanted, his eyes became soft. He had the kindest blue eyes that she had ever seen. He was so beautiful, this boy, the most beautiful boy in the world—and when she lifted up her face to his, he bent down to meet her halfway, his arms encircling her waist, holding her tightly.

It was just a kiss, but already she knew there would be more.

Ben murmured. "Took you long enough to come around, Legs."

"Mmm . . ." she agreed. She had wanted to take it slow. But what was the harm? He was only human. It was only a flirtation; at most he would end up her familiar. She had had many of those in her immortal lifetimes.

Allegra was still glowing from Ben's kiss when she returned to her dormitory, only to run into her brother.

"Where have you been?" Charles demanded. "I've been looking for you. You weren't at the Committee meeting tonight."

"Oh? Was that tonight? I forgot. I was busy."

"With what? Don't tell me you became a member of that asinine society of theirs?" he sneered.

"It's not stupid, Charlie. I mean, of course it's silly, but it's not stupid. There's a difference," she retorted.

"It's just a sad human copy of the Committee. We were here first."

"Maybe." She shrugged. "But they throw much better parties."

"What's happened to you?" Charles implored.

For a moment Allegra pitied him. "Nothing. Charlie. Please. Not here." She shook her head again.

"Allegra, we need to talk."

"There's nothing to talk about. What's there to talk about?"

"Cordelia . . . she's coming for Parents' Day on Sunday."

"Then tell Mother I said hello." With that, Allegra vanished into the dormitory without another word. The night had held so much promise. For a while there, joking around with the Peithologians, kissing Bendix, she had been able to believe that she was just an ordinary sixteen-year-old girl. But one conversation with Charles dispelled any remaining delusions that she might actually be able to have some fun in this lifetime.

## FIVE

## *His Mother's Son*

The only thing Charles Van Alen liked about his mother, his *cycle* mother, really, was that Cordelia was the only one in his life who did not call him by that stupid nickname.

"Charles, I was under the impression that your sister would be joining us today," she said as she poured him tea. It was Parents' Day, and the campus was empty, as the sponsors of the entire enterprise—those who paid the exorbitant tuition—came to visit their progeny and treat them to a meal at the town's more expensive dining establishments. Cordelia had arrived in a town car earlier that afternoon and taken Charles straight to high tea at the most prestigious hotel.

He leaned back in his uncomfortable chair. Why was it women insisted on this ridiculous practice? "I left her a note the other night to remind her. But she's been . . . preoccupied lately."

"Is that so?" Cordelia pursed her lips. She was small and birdlike, but her tongue was sharp; and even though she had diminished status in the Conclave, she still wielded enough power to have been assigned to foster him for this cycle. "Do tell, with what is our Allegra so distracted?"

Charles glowered. "She has a new boyfriend . . . one she might make a familiar." He would never admit to feeling jealousy over a Red Blood, but he couldn't take much more. First, her cool indifference. Now the unmistakable distaste. Allegra was slipping away from him, and he did not know why. He desperately wanted to hold on to her. It was the only thing he ever wanted.

But it seemed Allegra wanted the total opposite. *Leave me alone. Not here. Go away.* Those were the only words she ever said to him now. He couldn't stand it. It was as if she hated him. Why? What had he done? Nothing but love her. He did not want to admit to Cordelia that he did not know where she was spending the weekend, that he did not know where she was, and

70

he was damned if he was going to sink to the level of using the glom to try to find out. Allegra was his heart. She should come to him. She should want to be with him. And yet she did not. She made that all too clear.

"It's a mere infatuation. Just the bloodlust. Nothing to worry about," Cordelia assured. "You should let her be. She's had a hard time of it."

Charles knew what his mother meant—that Gabrielle needed time to heal. Even though Florence was but a distant memory, the pain from it—the ghastly action he had taken—of course, Lawrence was to blame, too—still lingered. It had been almost five hundred years already. Would she never be the same? She didn't even know the whole truth of it.

"The more you squeeze, the more she will squirm. It is best to let her make her own choice. She *will* choose you."

"There's something different about it this time," he said doubtfully, stirring his tea. "I fear that . . . she might actually love this one."

"Nonsense. He's human. It's nothing. You know that," Cordelia argued. "It's just a bit of fun. She'll come back to you. She always does. Trust me on this one,

Charles. You must let it run its course. Do not interfere; it will only lead to more estrangement between the two of you. Allegra needs her freedom right now."

"I hope you're right, Mother," Charles said darkly. "I shall stand aside for now. But if you're wrong about this, I shall never forgive you."

## SIX

## The Familiar's Kiss

Girls were not allowed in the boys' dorms after hours, and Allegra had to sneak in through the fire exit. It was easy enough to jump from the ladder to the ledge and knock on the windowsill.

"How'd you get up here?" Bendix asked, helping her inside. "That's not an easy climb."

She smiled. It was easy enough for a vampire, but of course he could not know that. She looked around his room, which was a tornado as usual. Boys. "Where's your roommate?"

"I sent him out. I had a feeling you were coming to visit." He smiled, walking over to the stereo to put on some music. None of that Grateful Dead stuff or Van

Morrison, thank goodness. It was Miles Davis. *Bitches Brew*.

Allegra sat on his bed, feeling shy suddenly. Even though they had kissed enough times over the course of a month that her mouth regularly felt bruised as a fruit, she still felt nervous about what she was about to do. So instead of looking at him, she investigated his bookshelves. There was a print on his wall. Not a poster. A lithograph. "You like Basquiat?"

"He's bit overhyped right now, but yeah."

"Didn't take you for a collector."

"I guess you just don't know me that well," he said, sitting on the office chair at his desk. He was wearing a white lacrosse T-shirt and boxer shorts, and his hair was wet from a shower.

"What are you doing way over there?" she asked, patting the empty space next to her.

He moved to sit next to her, and they snuggled together; and she pulled him close so she could smell the wonderful, boyish smell of him, of laundry detergent and Ivory soap and just a hint of aftershave.

"Hey," Ben said, hovering over her. He removed his T-shirt, tossing it to the side of the room. His chest was broad, hard to the touch, sculpted and defined.

Allegra thrilled to run her hands over his skin.

She was about to remove her top when he stopped her. He took her hands and gently pushed them away, and then with his teeth he unbuttoned each of her pajama buttons. She laughed when he looked surprised to see a camisole underneath.

"Tricky."

"I thought it shouldn't be too easy, right?"

"Hmmm."

He pushed off the straps of the camisole and then his head was on her chest, and she tugged him forward so that her hand was on the waistband of his shorts. She kissed his neck and his chest and felt the entire length of his body press against hers, and she wrapped her legs around his waist.

Neither of them spoke, and then Allegra whispered, "There's something you don't know about me."

"What's that?" he asked huskily.

This was it. It was time. This was what she had come to his room to do. She lifted up his chin so that he could see her clearly. Then she bared her fangs.

He looked at them in wonder but without fear. "You're a . . ."

"Vampire. Yes. You're not afraid?"

"No." He shook his head. "Maybe I should be, but I feel like . . . I'm looking at the real you. Like I'm seeing who you really are, for the first time. And you're beautiful. More beautiful, if that's even possible."

"When a vampire takes first blood, she marks her human as her familiar. You would be . . . mine," she explained. God, she wanted him so much. She could smell his blood underneath his skin, could already tell that it was going to be delicious and full of life—full of his unique and vital life force. She wanted him to be part of her, she wanted to be inside him and of him. She wanted him now.

"Legs, are you asking me to go steady?" he joked.

"It's more than that," she said gently. "You would be mine your entire life. You would never love another." Why was she telling him all the secrets of the Sacred Kiss? Just bite him and get it over with. And yet she wanted to—she wanted to give him a chance. A chance to choose his own destiny. "It's not going to hurt," she said.

"Oh, but I kind of want it to," he said, gazing up at her. "Hurt me, please."

"This isn't a joke, Ben. Do you really want me to . . . ?"

He nodded. He had chosen. "I'm up for it. Whatever it is. As long as it means I'll always be with you."

She kissed the base of his neck. She paused for a moment and let her fangs tease him, pricking his skin. She felt his excitement build, and at the right moment, she bit him as hard as she could. He clenched underneath and pulled her closer, his hands on her waist and their bodies joined together.

She drank his blood.

It was wonderful, more wonderful than she had imagined. It was glorious and she saw his every memory, learned his every secret—not that he had too many—he was an open book—filled with light and love—

Then something terrible happened.

Everything was wrong. The blood—what was in his blood? Dear God—what was this? Poison? Had he already been marked by another vampire? It could not be—she hadn't seen any of the signs, nothing to indicate that . . .

No. It wasn't poison.

It was a vision from the glom.

She saw . . .

*She was holding a baby girl in her hands. It was her daughter. . . . She caught a glimpse of her name . . . Schuyler? Where had she heard that name before? She was filled with joy and light and happiness . . . she had never felt happier in her life, or more alive, and next to her, she looked up and Ben was holding her hand and smiling, but then . . .*

*There was a second image . . . a few years later. . . .*

*She was lying in a hospital bed. She was comatose, the doctor was saying. There was no chance of recovery. Next to her, Charlie was sobbing. His hair was black, with silver streaks. No chance of recovery? But why? What had happened? What was happening? And where was Ben?*

*Why was she lying on the hospital bed? What was wrong with her? Was she dead? But vampires did not die. So what then—what had happened? And that terrible anguish on her brother's face. She had never seen him look so wretched.*

*And where was her baby? Where was her beautiful black-haired baby? The baby with Charles's dark hair and Ben's blue eyes. Where was her beautiful daughter? Where was her husband?*

*What was this?*

*What was she seeing?*

*Her future?*

She wrenched away. Back to the boys' dormitory, where she was straddling her first familiar.

"Don't stop. . . ." Bendix looked at her through a dreamy haze. He was already feeling the soporific effects of the *Caerimonia Osculor*. "Why did you stop . . . ?" he whispered. Then he was asleep.

Allegra put her clothes back on and gathered her things. What had she seen? What had just happened? All she knew was she had to get out of there as quickly as possible.

SEVEN

*Love Sick*

For two weeks, Allegra would not leave her bed, nor would she accept any visitors. She refused to eat, she refused to go to class, and rebuffed every entreaty—from her teachers, her resident adviser, her roommate, her teammates. The field hockey championships came and went without Allegra's involvement (Endicott lost, 4–2). She did not want to see anybody. Especially Ben, who had sent dozens and dozens of roses and left countless messages on the answering machine. Instead, she spent the hours lying huddled underneath her flowered comforter, alone and in despair. She had no idea what had come over her, only that she could not face her life. She could not face Ben. She did not want to think about anything. She just wanted to sleep. Or lie awake in the dark.

Finally, she allowed one visitor into her chamber.

Charles sat on the butterfly chair across from the bed and regarded his sister with a wary eye. He remained silent for a long time, taking in her matted hair, the dark circles under her eyes, the bluish color on her lips that meant she was dehydrated. The *sangre azul* was keeping her alive, but just barely.

"You did this to me," Allegra rasped. "This is your fault." It had to be the only explanation. Only Charles was powerful enough to have done it. There had to be a reason for what happened. It had to be Charles.

"I have no idea what you are talking about," he said, leaning forward. "Allegra. Look at you. What's happened?"

"You poisoned his blood!" she accused him.

"I did no such thing. And if his blood was marked, you would be in the hospital, not here." He stood up and opened the curtains to let light into the room. Allegra cowered from the sudden brightness. "Is that what happened? You took the human as a familiar?" He clenched his fists, and she could see the effort it took for him to say those words.

"Swear you had nothing to do with it," she said. "Promise me."

Charles shook his head. He looked sadder than she had ever seen him. "I would never harm anyone whom you cared for, and I would never stand in the way of your . . . happiness. I only wish you did not think so little of me."

She closed her eyes and shuddered. He was telling the truth. And if Charles was telling the truth, then she had to face the truth. That her vision was a warning.

"What did you see, Allegra?"

She turned toward the wall and away from him. She couldn't tell him. She wouldn't. It was too horrible.

"What is scaring you so much?" he asked tenderly. Charles knelt by her bedside and clasped his hands.

Allegra closed her eyes and saw the terrifying vision again. She knew now what it meant. In the dream, she was not dead. She was asleep. She would sleep for years. A decade and more. She would wither and sleep, and her daughter would grow up without a mother. Her daughter would grow up alone, an orphan, another ward taken under Cordelia's care.

As for Ben—what had happened to him? What did it mean that he was not in her second vision? Because she was sure he was the father of her child. Her baby had his kind blue eyes. He was there at the birth. Allegra's heart was certain even if her head screamed at the impossibility. She would bring their child into the world. A Half-Blood. Abomination. A sin against the Code of the Vampires. A code she had helped establish and enforce. The vampires were not given the gift of creating life; that blessing was reserved to the human children of the Almighty. And yet it had happened . . . but how?

Somewhere in the depths of her soul and her blood, she knew the answer. It lay somewhere in her past . . . in a past life that she could not bear to remember.

What would happen to Ben? Would Charles kill him? Where was he? Why was he missing in the second vision?

She had never seen anything like this before. She did not have the gift of sight, like the Watcher.

Charles reached for her hand. "Whatever it is, whatever happened, whatever you saw, there is nothing to fear. You have nothing to fear from me. Ever," he whispered. "You know that. . . ."

"Charlie . . ." she sighed, opening her eyes.

"Charles."

"Charles." She looked at him, at his blue-gray eyes, shaded by his thick black hair. Finally, she told him what she believed, what she had felt for so long, and had kept bottled up inside. "I don't deserve your love. Not anymore. Not since . . ."

He shook his head slowly. "Of course you do. You have been mine since time eternal. We belong together." He tightened his grip on her hand, but it was a gentle strength, not a possessive one.

Then Allegra finally understood. There was a way to stop this. To stop the downward spiral she had witnessed. To stop the terrible future from happening. To keep Bendix alive. For in the second vision, she knew, she *knew* he was dead. She had to stop the tragedy that was sure to unfold if she continued to love her human familiar. For it was love she felt for Bendix, she knew that now, had recognized it for what it was. Not the mere bloodlust that kept a vampire connected to her familiar, but love. Her own blood, the immortal blue blood in her veins, had tried to stop her from feeling this way. Had conjured up a vision of the future, to show her what would happen, should this love hold.

Her love would ruin her. Would ruin everything. Would take his life and hers and leave their daughter alone and defenseless in the world.

She did not have to love Bendix. She did not have to end up comatose and useless. Her daughter—she felt a piercing sadness, as if she were missing a daughter who had yet to be born—her daughter would never exist. It would never happen.

There was a way out of it. She could bond with Charles. She could take her rightful place at his side as his Gabrielle once more. In that moment, she accepted it, the weight of it—their history, the safety of the Coven, their legacy; she was their Queen and their Savior. She felt, for a moment, like her old self again. She had been running so fast in the other direction, she had forgotten there was nowhere in the universe she could run to that could keep her from what she had to do. Her duty.

She decided right then she would never see Bendix again. To protect him, to protect herself, she had to say good-bye. It was over. She would always love him, but she would do nothing to act on this love. In time, she would forget. She had all the time in the world.

Charles was still holding her hand.

She had been wrong to dismiss Charles, to push him away, to cringe at his touch. She saw that now. His eternal love was not a burden, it was a gift. She owned his heart. It was a responsibility she could live up to. She would keep it safe.

She touched his cheek tenderly. *Michael.*

It was all she had to send, and he understood.

# RING
## OF FIRE

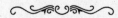

Florence

December

# ONE

## *Something Blue*

*S*chuyler Van Alen never thought of herself as the bridal type, so she was bemused to find herself the center of attention at the elegant dress shop she visited that morning. If at first she had felt intimidated and out of place in the hushed store, with marble floors and muted lighting, the friendly saleswomen soon put her at ease. They were more than eager to help once she told them what she was looking for. Everyone loved a wedding, and Florence was one of the most romantic places in the world to have one.

They had only been in the city a few days but Schuyler already knew her way around, using the towering marble basilica of the Duomo and the arches of the Ponte Vecchio as guideposts to figure out where she was in the city. She felt as if she had stepped onto a movie set. Florence was not just beautiful, but cinematic, with sweeping vistas thrumming with grandeur, and since it was November, the twisting streets were cold and relatively empty of art-loving tourists, which lent it a slightly melancholy air.

All week, Jack had been mysterious and tight-lipped, and he had hurried away that morning without telling her where he was going. Schuyler let him keep his secrets; she had her own surprise to plan. Even if theirs would be a simple ceremony, a world away from the grand occasion at the Cathedral of Saint John the Divine in New York City that Mimi's bonding planner had orchestrated, Schuyler still felt the intense and incredibly feminine need to make it special. She could not get bonded without a proper bonding dress. Her bank accounts were still untouchable—the Committee had seen to that—but Jack would not begrudge her the cost of a dress, she knew.

"What is your dream dress?" the doting saleslady asked in imperious Italian, glancing at Schuyler's outfit with a critical eye, taking in the old Converse sneakers, faded jeans, and wrinkled men's Oxford button-down.

"Romantic? Classic? Bohemian? Sexy?" Without waiting for an answer, the dowager snapped her fingers, and soon an army of clerks marched a succession of wedding gowns into the dressing room, each more beautiful and more intricate than the last.

As a child, Schuyler had never spun sugarplum dreams about her wedding, had never staged ornate romantic fantasies that included the exchange of vows with a giggly girlfriend pretending to be the teenage heartthrob of the day. Weddings required elaborate preparation and grandiose plans. It was a day that promised to transform an ordinary girl into a princess, and Schuyler had never had particularly royal ambitions.

She tried on the first dress, with a lushly embroidered bodice and a ten-foot train. When she looked at herself in the mirror, she remembered all those Upper East Side bondings her grandmother had dragged her to. They were always the same: cookie-cutter brides in their exquisite lace gowns or oceans of tulle, the grooms interchangeable, dashing and confident in black tie. The ceremony itself, she realized now, was not dissimilar from a common Red Blood union with their long-winded speeches, the mandatory reading from Paul's first letter to the Corinthians (Love is patient, love is kind, weddings are boring), the exchange of vows and rings. Afterward, if the family still kept up with the ways of the Old Coven, the receptions were tasteful and restrained, the elegant crowd jitterbugging to the Lester Lanin Orchestra; if they were distinctly New Coven types, the parties would be bombastic and flashy, with nightclub singers and a camera crew documenting the whole bedazzled, glittering mess.

"No, this one is too busy for you, *signorina*," the saleslady clucked, thrusting a different dress in her direction. This one was simple and backless, but when Schuyler put it on, she felt as if she were trying to be someone else. And on her bonding day she wanted most of all, to look like herself, only a little better.

Like many girls, she had taken it for granted that she would get married—one day—in the future—to someone. Didn't everyone get married? But it had never crystallized into a real desire, or intent, or focus. She was much too young, in the first place. She had just turned seventeen. But this was no ordinary bonding, and these were strange times. Most of all, she had pledged her heart to an extraordinary boy.

Jack Force was more than she had ever dared wish for, and he was better than a dream or a fantasy because he was real. He was far from perfect, moody and distant at times, and burdened with a sharp temper and an impulsiveness that was part of his dark nature. But she felt more love for him than she thought possible. He wasn't perfect, but he was perfect for her.

Schuyler allowed the helpful salesladies to talk her into trying on another dress, this one a tight strapless column with a row of minuscule buttons down the back. As nimble fingers latched every hook, she ruminated on how Jack's proposal had been a surprise, even if she had expected it. She was unprepared that it had happened so soon, but she understood the urgency. They had precious little time together. In a few days he would leave to return to New York, to face his fate, and afterward she might never see him again. She tried not to dwell on her fears, and instead focused on the brief moment of happiness they would be allowed before they would be separated again.

As for the bonding itself, they decided to keep it a secret from the Petruvians at the monastery. They did not know if they trusted the priests, and it was not an event they wanted to share with strangers. Schuyler had only a hazy idea of what Jack had planned. He had mentioned something about an old church in a far corner of the city, and a ceremony by candlelight. That was all she knew, except that there would never be a better time or place for this moment. It was all they had.

*"Bellissima!"* the sales team cooed as Schuyler apprised herself in the mirror. The dress hugged her in all the right places, and it was stunning.

However, it was not quite right. It was too formal somehow. She shook her head sadly. She thanked and hugged each of the saleswomen and exited the shop empty-handed.

Schuyler visited a host of dress shops on the plaza but found nothing that worked. The dresses were all too beaded, or too voluminous, too corseted, or too revealing. She wanted something simple and clean, a dress that promised fresh beginnings but also hinted at the swoon of surrender. She was about ready to give up the search—surely Jack would not care what she wore, would he?—could she make do with what she already had?—maybe that white cotton sundress?—when she found a small fabric shop tucked away in a dim alley by the Ponte Vecchio.

The elderly shopkeeper smiled. "How can I help you, *signorina*?"

"Could I see that? On the top shelf over there?" Schuyler asked, pointing to a bolt of fabric that had caught her eye the minute she entered the shop.

The old woman nodded and climbed the creaky ladder to bring it down. She laid it on the counter and unwrapped it slowly. "It is a rare Venetian silk, made by artisans from Como, the same way since the thirteenth century," the shopkeeper told her.

"It's beautiful," Schuyler whispered. She touched it reverently. It was a fine silk, soft and supple, light and airy to the touch. She had thought she would wear white—she was not so contrarian as to think she would get bonded in anything else. Yet the fabric she had chosen was the palest shade of blue. To the naked eye it looked ivory, but once you took a closer look you could see the hint of cobalt under the light.

Hattie had taught her a little about dressmaking, and the moment Schuyler saw the cloth she knew it was what she had been looking for all day. She paid for the fabric, her heart beating, her cheeks flushed with excitement at the task at hand. When she returned to their quarters that evening, Jack was still away. She borrowed needle and thread from the supply cabinet and started to work. First she cut a pattern on the muslin: the dress would be off-the shoulder, peasant-style, then drape and flow to the ground. That was all.

As she stitched, she sewed all her wishes and dreams into the dress, threaded there by her blood and her love. She felt a profound sense of joy and anticipation. Not for the first time, Schuyler wondered how she could be so lucky.

When she was done, her fingers were sore and her arms were tired. Night had come, but Jack had not yet returned. She took off her clothes and tried on the dress. The silk felt like water to the touch. She faced her reflection in the mirror with some trepidation, worried about what she might find. What if she had chosen wrong? What if Jack did not like it? What if it didn't fit correctly?

No. She had nothing to worry about. The muted blue color made her blue eyes shine even more brightly. It fell beautifully off her shoulders, and she decided she would wear her hair down.

It was the first time that Schuyler understood that she was actually going to be a bride. She clapped her hands to her mouth and tried to hide her smile. But it was too much—the happiness bubbled inside her, and she twirled in front of the mirror, laughing.

The sound of footsteps made her stop. Jack. He had returned. Quickly, she took off her bonding dress, hung it carefully in the back of her closet, and put her old clothes back on.

She did not believe old wives' tales, but she did not want him to see her in her dress until their bonding. Maybe she was a tiny bit superstitious after all.

# Two

## *Dark Circle*

*T*hey had been together for only a few months, but Schuyler knew the sound of Jack's step by heart, and something about the footsteps approaching the room sounded strange—as if someone was trying too hard to *sound* like Jack. She was instantly on alert, and removed her mother's sword from its hidden sheath, grasping its jeweled handle tightly. She stood by the side of the door and waited. The footsteps stopped abruptly, and there was only silence. She sensed that whoever was outside that door knew that she was aware of the deception, and she slowed down her breathing and calmed her nerves.

When the door opened, its centuries-old hinges

turned without creaking, and Schuyler realized her unwanted visitor had set a spell of silence around the room. No one would be able to hear her scream for help. Not that she needed any. She could defend herself. When the tip of a sword appeared at the opening, she held her breath and steadied her hand, ready to attack.

A black-clad Venator entered the room, stepping soundlessly toward her across the rough wood floors. The black-and-silver cross on his clothing marked him as one of the Countess's men, and Schuyler felt absurdly thankful that he was not from the New York Coven.

She lifted her weapon. The Venators' relentless pursuit had added misery upon misery to her life. She never felt safe anywhere, and the opportunity to finally face that fear and fight a hidden and unstoppable enemy came as a relief.

The man in black swung wide with his sword, and she managed to block his blow even as his reach exceeded hers by more than a foot. A simple swordfight would not end in her favor, and Schuyler circled the room for a moment, tracing a path just outside of his weapon's reach. If she fought this battle on his terms, she would be his captive in mere moments.

The Venator attacked again; but instead of meeting

his parry, Schuyler jumped up and landed on a wood truss that crossed the room's high cathedral ceiling. Safe for a moment, she looked down at her foe. He crouched in preparation to leap; but before he could fly, Schuyler slashed fiercely at the wooden trusses holding her. The heavy timber split like soft twigs, sending the massive beams collapsing down on the Venator. She leapt from beam to beam, breaking the trusses, and the wooden shards rained down to the floor, splinters shattering in all directions.

The destruction would have raised a ruckus large enough to wake the entire city had it not been for the *silentio*. The roof heaved, but held. Meanwhile, the Venator had managed to climb on top of the woodpile and was closing in fast. Schuyler turned back quickly and cut the nearest post to its base, sending it flying toward her attacker.

The Venator looked up just as the first shards bit into his shoulder. With inhuman speed, he stopped it from crushing him by driving his blade into the heavy wood. Now was her chance. Schuyler leapt toward the Venator, and the force of her left foot crashed on his clasped hands, pushing them against the hilt of his sword in the opposite direction until the weapon snapped in half.

Schuyler drew her own sword and pressed it to his neck.

"Surrender!" she demanded, her voice echoing through the room. She had broken the spell when she had broken his blade.

The Venator only regarded her with contempt. "You can slay me, but doing so will doom your friend." He lifted his hand and turned his palm to reveal a Venator stone, hanging on a chain—and inside the stone was an image.

The stone showed Oliver Hazard-Perry, blindfolded and bound.

Schuyler gasped. "This is a trick. Oliver is back in New York. . . ." she said, keeping her sword at his neck.

"He arrived in Italy a half an hour ago. We caught him in the airport."

"But why would he be in Italy unless . . ." And then Schuyler realized: Jack's mysterious errands. The other night when he had asked her what she wanted most for their bonding, she had told him that she only wished her friends could be there on the most important day of her life. She had told him she knew it was impossible and that it was silly of her to wish for something she could not have. Oliver was working for the Repository back in New York, and who knew where Bliss had gone.

But Jack had made it happen. Her love had invited her friends to their bonding.

Her heart melted a little, but her happiness at discovering Jack's secrets had to wait. Oliver was a hostage. Her dear sweet friend—she felt a lump in her throat when she thought of the extent of his generosity. He had come to her bonding to celebrate. He had arrived as a guest only to become a victim.

Schuyler kept her sword at the Venator's throat. "What do you want for his life?"

The Truth Seeker smiled. "I knew you would come around. This could have been accomplished without all this ruckus." He removed a velvet pouch from his pocket and shook out a white metal ring. "Give this to Abbadon," he directed, and whispered a few words into her ear. "Make sure he wears it always."

"What will it do?" Schuyler asked, staring at the ring.

"The spell will keep him from being able to express his true nature. When we meet again, he will not be able to overpower us, and we will have both of you in our custody. Your love for Abbadon is molded into the ring. As long as your love for him holds, the ring will keep his power in check."

She balked. The ring had the power to turn the deepest, most important part of her soul into a restraint, a handcuff. They meant to trap Jack with her true love for him. "No. I cannot. I will not."

"You will do as told, or I will make certain that your friend not only perishes, but that his death is long and painful. If you tell Abbadon the truth, if you try to find help, your friend will die immediately. Take the seeing stone and wear it around your neck. It will enable us to see what you see and hear what you say, even in the glom. Give Abbadon the ring. Or sacrifice your friend. We will be watching."

Then, with a few words, the Venator restored the room to its former, uncluttered state.

# THREE

## *Reunion*

*T*he man in black disappeared out the window just as the door opened again. This time it was Jack who entered. Schuyler hurriedly put away the ring in the velvet pouch, but as the Venator had instructed, wore the seeing stone around her neck.

Jack had a worried look on his handsome face, and sat on the bed with a heavy sigh as he removed his boots.

"What's wrong?" Schuyler asked, moving to kneel behind him so that she could gently rub his shoulders. His muscles felt tight and strained, and she worked her fingers on the knots.

"The Countess's Venators will be here soon. I fear

the Petruvians have betrayed us," he told her.

"Ghedi?" she asked, alarmed.

"No—he is a friend. He was the one who warned me. But the bonding cannot wait until Saturday. We must leave as soon as we can. They will be upon us if we do not move."

If only she could tell him the Venators had already found them.

"I'm sorry," he said, turning to her and reading the distress on her face. "I know it's not the kind of news a bride wants to hear before her bonding."

"No, no . . . it's not that. . . ." She wanted to tell him everything, but she did not have a choice. She would have to do what the Venator had ordered her to do. Oliver would die if she did not. She removed the velvet pouch from her pocket and, as if in a dream, she offered it to Jack.

"What's this?" he asked.

Her hands shook. "I wanted to wait and give you this at the bonding, but since we have so little time . . . Will you wear this for me now?"

In answer, Jack held out his hand with a broad smile, and she slipped the ring on his finger. She whispered the words the Venator had ordered her to say.

"This ring is a symbol of my faithfulness, it binds you to me, and my love shall hold you always."

There. She'd done it.

She held his hand for a long moment, and with her finger traced two circles under his palm. The gesture was part of the code they had developed when they had been under the Countess's "protection." The two circles meant that they were being watched. They had developed the secret signs in order to communicate with each other and plan their escape while under the Venators' guard.

Jack looked at the ring on his finger but his face betrayed nothing. Did he understand what she had just told him? Did he remember their code? He had to.

Oliver's life depended on it.

A knock on the door interrupted them. "Jack? Schuyler? You have a visitor," Ghedi said. They exchanged a wary glance. Schuyler steeled herself—had the Venators come back so soon? But when the door opened, the face that appeared was so beloved and familiar that she immediately rushed to greet the new arrival. "Bliss!"

"Sky!" Bliss Llewellyn burst into the room, her copper tresses bouncing. She moved with a new vibrancy, and Schuyler was glad to see her friend looking so well—there was color in her cheeks and her green eyes sparkled with life. There was something different about her—her arms did not bear the telltale sign of the *sangre azul*. She did not know what happened to Bliss, only that her friend had survived the darkness that had tried to claim her as its own. Bliss had come out on the other side, looking better than ever; and for that Schuyler was thankful.

She hugged her friend tightly. "You're here."

"Of course. Once Jack said you guys were getting bonded, how could I not be here for you?" Bliss smiled. "I know this was supposed to be a surprise, Jack, but I'm sorry, I couldn't wait. I have awful news."

"What's wrong? What's happened?" Schuyler asked, but she had an inkling that she already knew.

Bliss crossed her arms. "I saw Oliver at customs, and we were supposed to meet up at baggage claim to catch a cab to the hotel together. I waited for him and he never showed. I looked around and I felt like I was being watched. Venators, by the looks of them. They were everywhere. I managed to slip away, but I think they got Oliver." Bliss explained that she and Jane Murray had been in Chicago when Jack had called.

Since she was supposed to be gone for only a few days, she had left the Watcher to stay on the trail of the Hellhound they had been tracking. "Do you know why they would take him?"

"It's the European Coven. They're after us," Schuyler explained. "The Countess wants us dead. She's still loyal to her brother—Lucifer."

Bliss nodded to indicate she understood. They were never too far from the threat of the Morningstar—she knew better than most.

"Schuyler, can you find Oliver in the glom? We need to see where he's being held, and you carry his blood. You should be able to find him faster than I," Jack said.

Schuyler closed her eyes. She knew Jack was right, but she had a feeling they were walking into a trap. The Venators *wanted* them to find Oliver. They were being jerked around like puppets, but she had no other options. She couldn't tell Jack what had happened earlier, about the danger that came from the ring he wore on his finger. She could only trust that he remembered the meaning behind her signal, and that somehow, they would be able to outsmart the Venators. They had done it before.

She reached out into the spirit world, searching for her friend and former familiar. *Ollie . . . where are you? Can you hear me?* No harm could come to him, not to Oliver, not to Bliss, not to her dear friends who had come to Italy for the purpose of celebrating her bonding. Whatever happened, Schuyler promised she would keep them safe.

*Oliver?*

*I'm here.*

*Are you all right?*

*For the moment. Where are you?*

*Coming to get you.*

Schuyler opened her eyes. "They're holding him in the Villa Malavolta, the old Villa Feri. In the tower room."

"I will go," Jack said, putting on his jacket.

Schuyler shook her head. "Not alone. We'll come, too."

"You'll need us," Bliss agreed. "Even if I'm just human now." She waved off their confusion. "I'll explain later. It's a long story."

Jack turned to Schuyler and shook his head. "I cannot risk it." *I cannot risk you.*

"Jack," Schuyler said softly. She took his hand, and

glanced again at the traitorous ring he wore on his finger. "I am already in danger, my love, and you cannot protect me always. I can protect myself."

And I need to be there to protect you, she thought, but could not say or send, lest the Venators hear.

# FOUR

## *Lord of the Underworld*

*J*ack knew he could not argue Schuyler out of joining the rescue party. He was glad she had Bliss with her—it would help to have a friend fighting by her side. Not that anything was going to happen, of course; he was going to make sure of it.

He pointed to the ceiling. "They're right above us."

The three of them had raced through the city's ancient underground tunnels toward the intersection of Via del Podestà and Via Bernardo Martellini. The Florentine maze was identical to the one in Lutetia, and Jack had maneuvered through the twists and turns with ease. The building had been owned since the early fifteenth century by the same Blue Blood family that had

111

close ties to the Medicis, but had recently been sold to an unknown bidder. Unlike most buildings in Florence, the villa had a basement so that its first floor would be symmetrical to the road. The tunnels led directly to its basement, and they had arrived in mere moments.

Now they were underneath the room where Oliver was being held. While there was no way to enter the room in the physical world without breaking through to the floor above, there were no such barriers in the glom. Once Jack was in the twilight world, he would be in the same space as the Venators. He could attack without even entering the room.

"It sounds like there are hundreds of them up there," Schuyler said.

Jack nodded. It was the perfect plan. As Abbadon, he would subdue the Venators in the glom, while Schuyler and Bliss rescued Oliver in the physical world.

"Jack . . ." Schuyler said. She bit her lip. "Be careful."

He squeezed her shoulder. "Don't worry. I'll be back soon."

Jack Force moved into the glom. Schuyler was right: he had sensed the presence of more than a hundred Venators guarding the former Conduit in the physical world. Yet only three of the Truth Seekers were posted in the glom.

Strange that his enemies had chosen to keep their forces gathered in the tangible universe. Surely they knew Abbadon would attack in the twilight world first. Which meant the Venators did not fear his strength in the glom. But why?

Jack hunched downward, clenching his fists.

The first Venator dove headlong toward Jack, wielding a black sword. Jack met the man's thrust by grabbing the Venator's wrist and turning the blade toward the Venator's own body. He used the momentum of the Venator's own charge against him and drove the blade right into his opponent's knee, splitting the flesh and tearing the joint wide. The Venator rolled sideways in agony as he drifted out of the glom. The remaining two formed a tight circle around Jack.

They attacked in unison this time, one advancing from the front while the other slid toward him from the rear. Jack preempted their attack, leaping backward to smash into the attacker's chest. The move was unexpected, and he hit the man hard before the Venator had drawn his blade. His adversary reeled to the ground, stunned.

Jack's unexpected leap kept him clear of the third Venator's advance for a moment, and he took the opportunity to remove the sword from the Venator's fallen comrade before the man slipped out of the glom. Jack swung the blade in a tight arc, feeling the weight of the sword, sensing its internal balance and strength.

He tossed the weapon to his other hand and traced a line inches from the Venator's chest. "Call your friends. They were arrogant to have sent only three men when a hundred wait in reserve. Call them all if you think you have a chance of taking me tonight."

Jack held the man's gaze and did not blink. He waited until the Venator disappeared from the glom before relaxing his hand.

*Would they take the bait?* Their plan would only work if Jack could draw all of them into the glom and away from the room where they held Oliver.

Jack waited in the void of the glom, tense and alone. He balanced his sword in readiness. Where were they?

Finally, the first Venator blinked into the spirit world.

Jack raised his sword and then raised it higher as more and more of them appeared. He had miscalculated.

There were more than a hundred of them. Their numbers were astounding. Almost all of the Venators in service to the European Coven had to be here. The Countess wanted her revenge very dearly, it was clear.

He was surrounded. Jack did the only thing he could—he lowered his weapon. It was useless against a group of this size. The Venator army closed in tightly around him. Their faces were calm. They had no fear. Their numbers were vast, their strength overwhelming.

"Surrender, Abbadon! Your defeat is guaranteed." The words came from a vampire Jack did not recognize. The Venator that led this army had been nothing more than a foot soldier in the celestial army Jack had commanded long ago.

This was going to be too easy, really. He began the transformation into his true form, calling up the immortal spirit that was housed in his blood for time immemorial. Abbadon, the Unlikely. Angel of the Apocalypse. Destroyer of Worlds.

But nothing happened. No dark wings sprouted from his back, no horns grew on his forehead, he was without the strength of a million demons coursing through his veins. He remained Jack Force. Just another eighteen-year-old boy.

*Ah.*

So that was their game.

He had guessed as much, the moment Schuyler had drawn those two circles on his palm. Had seen her hands shake as she had put the ring on his finger. They had placed a cursed bonding spell on them, to limit his powers. To stop him from turning into Abbadon. Held back by the love she felt for him. He had noticed that telltale stone around her neck, disguised as a pendant. They were watching, they were waiting. *This* is what they wanted him to do. They wanted him weak and vulnerable, bereft of his immortal power.

"Something wrong, Abbadon?" the Venator sneered. "Where is your strength now?"

Jack sighed. "Do you truly believe that brute force is my only weapon? That after centuries of rule in Heaven, I wield no power but my own sword?"

The Venator smirked. "What other power could you possibly still have? After today, they will call you Abbadon the Weak."

In reply, Jack spoke a small incantation, a prayer that only he could fashion. The glom darkened considerably, and from the fatal blackness arose the creatures of the Underworld, the Black Fire elementals at his

116

command, as one of the First Born, an Angel of the Dark, captain of the lost and withering souls of Hell.

Abbadon might be chained, but Jack still carried his spirit, and the primal creatures bowed to their master. He screamed as he drove his dark army into battle. How ironic that stripped of his power to transform, only then did he recall the breadth and depth of the darkness that had molded him. For too long he had not made use of the powers of the Dark, had not tapped into the deep, hidden strength of the Underworld where he had been made and his name forged in fire and death.

The dark creatures overpowered the Venators in strength and number. Jack pitied the Truth Seekers until he remembered Schuyler's anguished face from earlier that evening. The Countess had brought death and bloodshed to their bonding. That could not be helped now. He only hoped Schuyler had been able to carry out her part of the plan, that she and her friends were safe.

Jack looked down at the band of steel that was wrapped around his finger, dull and ordinary, even as its dark magic glowed with a fiery treachery.

chuyler shivered as Jack disappeared into the glom. He would be vulnerable in the glom, just as the Venators had wanted. What would become of him? She had to trust that he would be fine. That he could take care of himself, and that he had understood what she could not tell him.

Before they had set off, Jack had asked her to believe in him and follow their plan. He would draw all the Venators to the glom and take care of them there while she and Bliss freed Oliver. Jack had been clear about one thing: whatever happened, she had to trust him. Even if something happened that she did not understand. He had asked her to promise, and she had agreed.

"Ready?" she asked Bliss, looking up at the ceiling.

"Are you sure you can do this?" Bliss asked, looking doubtfully at the thick planks.

Schuyler thought back to her earlier encounter with the Venator. She had not known the full strength of her sword until the moment she had nearly hacked apart the entire roof structure without so much as breaking a sweat. "I think I can make a little hole in the floor." She smiled as she raised her sword to the floorboards above.

The blade carved a rough hole in the ceiling. Schuyler leapt through the gap and gazed down at Bliss. "Join me?" she asked. Bliss frowned and Schuyler realized she had forgotten that her friend now lacked the power she took for granted. "Sorry," she said as she reached down through the hole and lifted Bliss up into the room.

They found themselves staring at a sea of blank faces. Schuyler met the impassive gaze of the nearest Venator. He looked as if he were in a trance. Her heart raced. Jack's plan was working. He had drawn the Venators into the glom. Now it was her turn to complete the rescue.

"Let's split up, make sure they're all gone," Schuyler said.

They made their way through the catatonic crowd. When a person was in the glom, their body remained limp and motionless in the physical world. She looked into the eyes of each Venator she passed and saw Bliss doing the same. The army was defenseless. *Defenseless only if they had all moved into the glom*, she thought. She knew better than to believe that the Truth Seekers would leave themselves unprotected. There had to be someone here who was pretending, playing dead, playing possum. She had to find him before he found her.

"Umgghh."

The sounded echoed through the silent hall. It had to be Oliver. He was somewhere in the back, obscured by the mass of bodies. Schuyler and Bliss raced toward him from opposite sides of the room. Schuyler shoved right and left, pushing roughly through the somnolent Venators that had taken her friend hostage and threatened his life.

She found Oliver, gagged and tied to an old wooden chair.

Bliss arrived at the same time. She looked over her shoulder and said, "I think they're all out, Sky."

Gingerly, she poked one of the Venators on his shoulder while staring directly into his dead eyes.

"Keep looking; we are not alone. I'm sure of it," Schuyler said, as she ripped the gag from Oliver's mouth.

He let out a quick cough and took a deep inward breath before raising his head. "Thanks," he said softly. He looked around with tired eyes, confused. "Bliss, is that you?"

"The one and only." Bliss grinned. "Good to see you," she said, punching him on the shoulder.

"We need to get out of here," Schuyler said, as she cut the ropes binding Oliver's chest. "Can you walk?" she asked.

He lifted himself to his feet and nodded. She grabbed his hand and led the other two toward the hole in the floor.

"That was easy," Bliss said, as they shimmied through the unconscious army.

"Not quite," a voice said quietly.

Schuyler turned around. She recognized that voice.

One of the sleeping Venators lunged forward. It was the same one who had attacked her earlier.

"The three of you are going to help me end this," the

Venator said, and with a wave of his hand, everything went dark.

When Schuyler opened her eyes again, there was a wild howling in the background.

They were in the glom.

## SIX

*Abbadon's Curse*

*J*ack raised his fist, and the whirlwind of dark spirits paused for a moment. The shriek of their mad voices was deafening. Their twisted forms swirled in and out of focus, like some fearsome tornado writhing in all directions. He could feel the Venators' terror. The Truth Seekers were centuries old, veterans of conflicts both human and supernatural, but the creatures of the Dark were unmistakably horrific. He let the dark mass hover above them for a moment.

The terrifying howl was momentarily quiet as Jack focused on the Venator captain. Jack addressed the man who had mocked him earlier. "Let Oliver go and I will spare your army. You may return to the Countess with your men intact."

The commander grimaced. "There is no turning back for us, my friend. We were sent to retrieve you at any cost. You may have my army, but I have your friends."

In that instant, three figures materialized in front of them: Oliver, Bliss, and Schuyler, each guarded by a Venator. The one holding Schuyler held a sword that shone with the Black Fire. Since they were human, Oliver and Bliss looked a little green around the edges. As living spirits, humans could enter the glom, but their physical and psychological makeup made their experience in the twilight world akin to a bumpy ride. Side effects included vertigo and nausea.

The captain of the Venators smiled thinly. "Surrender, Abbadon. Let the Countess help you find your way back to the Morningstar."

"No—Jack, don't!" Schuyler cried. "Don't let them take you!"

So that was what Drusilla wanted. His former allegiance. A chance to redeem himself with his old master. For Lucifer had been his commander as well.

Jack shook his head slowly. The Dark had tremendous

power, but its strength was unfocused. The creatures could tear bodies and weapons with colossal ease, but would not be able to save his friends from a quick knife. He could not protect his friends. He could not protect his love. He knew what he had to do. He looked at the ring on his finger.

The Venator spoke again. "The choice is yours. Surrender to us, and we shall set them free. Fight, and they shall die."

Jack did not hesitate. He opened his fist and unleashed the wild fury of the Dark. He looked straight into his enemy's eyes as he roared, "THEN LET THEM DIE!"

Bliss screamed as Oliver swung wildly at the man that held him, punching him roughly in the chest. But Schuyler stood motionless for a moment.

She did not know what to believe. She had to trust Jack. She had to believe he was doing this for a reason. So she had to believe that sacrificing them was part of his plan. She had promised to trust him. No matter what happened. Even if something happened that she did not understand.

"Kill her first," Jack sneered, pointing at Schuyler. She stared at Jack's angry, contorted face. Schuyler held his gaze for a moment, and she shuddered to see so much hate in his eyes.

It was a trick; it *had* to be. He was lying. Wasn't he? She was about to panic but she forced herself to think it through. It had to be a lie, but for some reason Jack wanted her to believe he did not love her. Then she realized. Jack *knew*. He knew about the ring and the power it had over him, a power that was fueled by the deepest emotion in her soul: her love for him. She had to find a way to stop loving him. It was the hardest thing she had ever done, but she willed herself, she tricked herself into believing the lie. She believed it with all of her heart. *Jack did not love her. Jack had never loved her. Jack wanted her dead. Jack . . .*

And just as he wished, her love for him faltered for a moment.

The curse was broken, and the ring that held him fell to the ground smoking. The transformation was instantaneous. Jack vanished, and there was only Abbadon, the Angel of Destruction, rearing his ugly head, his dark wings beating against the wind.

With a ferocious strength, Abbadon grappled with the guard holding the black sword, and the weapon twisted under his mighty grip, shattering in midair.

Abbadon lifted the frail and confused Venator by the back of his neck and tossed him toward the dark whirlwind.

Schuyler acted just as quickly, turning to face the Venator whose appearance had begun this terror-filled night. She slid between Oliver and the Venator's blade, swinging low to parry his quick blow as they twisted weapons in midair. He tossed his dagger to the side and pulled a longer blade from its scabbard. But Oliver, tired of captivity, found new strength as a shot of adrenaline pulsed through his veins. He found the Venator's vulnerable side and delivered a powerful punch. The Venator turned to him swinging his blade, but Oliver's diversion left his right flank unprotected.

Schuyler swung at the open spot, her blade slashing deep into his armor. The Venator wrenched sideways, confused by the multiple blows, unnerved by the strength of her sword. He tried to balance himself, but a sudden, unexpected kick from Bliss sent him sprawling to the ground. He collapsed in defeat.

Schuyler doubled over, catching her breath, when Jack laid a tender hand on her shoulder. "It's done," he said. "We're safe. Let's go."

"Jack—" She could not find the words. Even if the battle had been won, she felt as if she had failed him. Even if it had been a trick, even if it had been something she'd had to do to restore his power, she wanted him to know that she had never stopped loving him. Not even for that instant. She had been able to trick the spell to break the curse, but her heart would always remain steadfast.

"I know," he said softly. "As I hope you know . . ."

"You don't have to say it," she whispered, tears springing to her eyes to see Jack's green eyes shining with their usual warmth again. It had been too frightening to believe in his anger and indifference. It spoke to her deepest fear—that Jack's feelings for her were false, that their love was all a dream. But now as he held her in his arms, she realized her fears were a dream, and it was their love that was true.

"I am sorry for putting you through that. Forgive me," he said, his face buried in her hair. His hand cupped the back of her head gently, but with the same possessive weight that always gave her a secret thrill.

She shook her head. It had been an ordeal, but one that they had faced together. Their friends were safe and their love was more powerful than any curse. Nothing could hold them back now.

When she blinked her eyes again, all of them were back in the physical world, in the tunnels under the villa.

# SEVEN

## *Dress Rehearsal*

"A toast," Oliver proposed, standing with his wineglass raised. There were only four of them at the table: the happy couple and their two friends who had traveled so far to be with them today. They had weathered violence and evil, and now they were ready to celebrate.

Schuyler beamed and leaned back against Jack, waiting to see what Oliver would say. After they had escaped from the Villa Malavolta, leaving the Countess's army of Venators a crumpled and disbanded heap and no longer a threat to anyone's safety, they had followed Jack back up to the city streets. They had seen their friends safely to their hotel, and after allowing a few hours to freshen up and recover from their latest adventure, they had agreed to meet at a local trattoria for dinner.

Oliver had taken her aside on the walk from the palazzo to the restaurant, linking arms with her. "He won't mind, will he?" he smiled, motioning to Jack.

Schuyler shook her head. "Of course not, Ollie. It's *so good* to see you," she said, giving his arm a squeeze. She marveled at the ease of their affection. When they had parted ways at the airport just a few months ago, she had wondered if she would ever see him again, and it made her heart swell to see him looking so happy and healthy. "You look different. You look better. What did the Venators *do* to you?" she joked.

"Nothing this old boy can't handle," he assured her. "But you're right. I am different."

He told her about Freya, the witch who had cured his heart and his blood. "I am no longer marked," he said.

"I felt it." She nodded. She scanned his open, friendly face. "I am so glad." They were back to their former allegiance, two friends, their emotions neatly organized back to the way it used to be. Oliver was right. It had to be magic.

131

"So is it serious?" she teased.

Oliver shook his head. "No. I'll probably never see her again, but it's okay. Don't you worry about me," he said, before planting a hearty kiss on her forehead.

"Hey!" Jack called. "Only the groom gets to kiss the bride!"

Schuyler and Oliver giggled, and they followed Jack and Bliss into the small café. When the manager found out it was a pre-wedding dinner, they were treated to a feast: steaming plates of tender beef carpaccio and grilled zucchini, white truffle carbonara, ravioli stuffed with pears and pecorino cheese, a buttery and tender Florentine steak. For dessert, there were plates of Sacher torte and tarte tatin and the best tiramisu Schuyler had ever tasted.

Now Oliver was standing in the middle of the restaurant, clearing his throat. "A toast," he said. "A toast to an amazing couple. I wanted to say something simple and elegant for this momentous occasion, so I'll leave it to the poets instead. This is a poem that was composed for a wedding." He began to read from a poem by Frank O'Hara. It was a winding tale of love and friendship, and the group listened keenly. "'This poem goes on too long because our friendship has been long,

long for this life and these times.'" Oliver smiled. "'And I would make it as long as I hope our friendship lasts if I could make poems that long.'"

"Hear, hear," Jack cheered, and Schuyler clinked his glass.

Oliver took his seat to wild applause, as even the rest of the restaurant's patrons had stopped to listen to the music of his words.

Bliss stood up next. "Ollie, you're a hard act to follow," she chided. She cleared her throat. "I just want to say how honored I am to be here today. We love you, Sky, and because we love Sky, we love you too, Jack. Take care of each other. Be kind to each other. You have all our good wishes and all of our hearts. Don't forget us and don't forget to ask for help when you need it." She paused, and for a moment Schuyler thought Bliss would talk about the many dangers they would soon be facing. Her friends knew that after the bonding, she and Jack would be separated, that this was just a small bubble, an oasis of happiness before a long and dark story of separation and unknown menace.

After tomorrow, the four of them would each set off from Italy on their own perilous journeys. Oliver back to New York, where vampires were being mysteriously abducted; Bliss to search for the elusive Hellhounds; Schuyler to Alexandria to fulfill her grandfather's legacy; and Jack to return to face his twin and his destiny, to see if he could win the battle with Death herself.

But Bliss did not mention any of the darkness. She did not have to: they were all thinking the same thing. In a clear voice, she called out, "To Schuyler and Jack!"

There was a bang of wineglasses and merrymaking. Bliss gave Schuyler a fierce hug. Schuyler pulled Jack into the embrace, and Bliss made room for Oliver, so that the four of them were linked in an unbroken circle.

## EIGHT

## *Wedding Morning*

arly the next morning in the privacy of their bed, Schuyler huddled closer to Jack. She could feel the sunlight streaming into the room, filling it with warmth. Today was their bonding day. She felt his hand on the small of her back, his skin on her skin as he slipped it underneath the light fabric. She turned to him so that she was enveloped, crushed in his arms.

Without saying a word, Jack began to kiss her cheek and her neck, and Schuyler felt his body move over hers, felt the heaviness of him settle upon her. After tonight, they would be bonded.

But that morning, they were still just two people.

After all those trysts in the secret apartment, one

would think they had already crossed this line. But she was still chaste. Still innocent, although perhaps not as naive as a virgin bride slipping into her wedding bed, nervous and shaking. No. Not *that* innocent. But she had wanted to wait for this, had wanted to wait until she was ready, and now she did not want to wait any longer.

She opened her eyes and found him staring at her. The question in his eyes was answered by her kiss. *Yes, my darling. Yes. Now.*

She lifted his shirt above his chest and helped him undress, her fingers lightly skimming the length of his body. He was so beautiful and warm and solid. And he was hers. She felt pliant and soft underneath him. His skin was hot to the touch, and it felt as if they were both burning, burning.

She could not breathe, she could not think, she could only feel—only feel his kiss and his touch and his weight and the two of them together.

Jack sank his fangs into her neck and she surrendered to him, to love, to pleasure, to the feel of him everywhere—in every last part of her. He took her and held her, and when it happened, she felt broken and free and new.

She could not stop crying. She was so happy, although happy was not the word, it was more than that. It was strong and coursing through her as if she were lit like a candle, an extension of his love and lust, a mere collection of nerve endings. She felt open and whole and surrendered.

"What is wrong, my love?" he whispered, his beautiful face a breath from hers.

She pulled him ever closer. She kissed him hungrily. *Nothing is wrong. Nothing . . . nothing at all.*

It was wonderful and frightening and awkward and ecstatic, and she was dizzy from the blood and the pain. But the pleasure was more intense, and more than she could have imagined.

Sweet oblivion.

Tonight they would be bonded. Tonight, she would be his. But she was already.

# NINE

## *Angel Bride*

At sunset, Schuyler walked into a small church on the north side of the city. She had made the journey alone, as tradition called, her new leather sandals stepping lightly on the cobblestones. When she arrived, Bliss was waiting for her at the vestibule entry.

"You look gorgeous as usual," her friend sighed. "And that dress!" Bliss handed her a bouquet of wildflowers. The same kind that Jack had given her during their climb up Mount Rosa. "Jack wanted me to give this to you."

Schuyler smiled as she accepted them. She put a flower in her hair. Her heart beat wildly, and she felt so

much love—not just for Jack but for her friends, who were with her on this night.

"Where's our girl?" a voice asked.

"Ollie!" Schuyler cried, turning to give him a tight hug. Even though they had just seen each other the night before, she was so glad that after everything they had gone through, they were all there for one another. This was what she had wanted. A bonding was both a commitment between her and Jack and a celebration for their community. These were her people.

"I think I get to give you away," Oliver said with a smile. "Which is only appropriate, don't you think?"

From behind the closed chapel doors, Schuyler heard the sound of Wagner's Bridal Chorus, commonly known as "Here Comes the Bride." A traditional choice perhaps, but on her bonding day Schuyler did not want to trifle with convention. She felt deep-seated desire to pay homage to the institution they were joining.

"I think that's our cue," she told Oliver, taking his hand. Bliss opened the doors and stepped into the aisle first, as the bridesmaid.

Schuyler felt none of the butterflies or anxiety she had thought she would feel. She looked straight ahead.

Because there he was.

Her Jack, standing so straight and true. Their love had been tested and challenged, but they had come out of it whole. Their love was stronger than ever. This bright, cheerful happiness that filled the room was his creation. He had cast his own spell, had managed to track down Bliss, and had brought Oliver from New York. They were not even the only friends in attendance. The small chapel was filled with smiling, familiar faces. There was the entire lacrosse team: Bryce Cutting and Jamie Kip and Booze Langdon and Froggy Kernochan. There were Hattie and Julius Jackson, beaming and proud. There was Christopher Anderson. There was Ghedi, their friend, even after everything.

Oliver kissed her on the cheek and shook Jack's hand.

Then Jack kissed her forehead, and the two of them walked toward the altar. This was right, this was wonderful. This was the happiest day of her life.

Somewhere, not too far, Schuyler felt the presence of those who were missing. She felt Dylan smiling. She felt the love of her grandparents, Lawrence and Cordelia. But most of all, she felt the loving presence and guardianship of her mother and father, wherever they were.

\* \* \*

There was no priest at the head of the altar. Blue Blood unions were made by the bondholders themselves. They only had to consecrate their union by saying the right words to each other.

Jack turned to Schuyler, reaching for her left hand. He slipped a ring on her finger. It was the same one that the Venator had brought. The cursed ring.

"Drusilla thought she could spoil this day for me. But she was wrong," Jack said. "I should thank her, truly, for giving back what I had once lost."

Schuyler stared curiously at the ring on her finger. The white metal was gone. She saw now that it was a dark-colored band, threaded with a crimson line, as if it were cast of iron and blood.

Jack held it up to the light.

*In all my years on this Earth, I have amassed a fortune of jewels and treasures. I can offer you diamonds and rubies, sapphires and emeralds. Yet there is no jewel brighter than your eyes.*

As he spoke, Schuyler realized he was opening a way to the glom, and when she blinked, the two of them were standing across from each other in the shadow world. The church and their friends had disappeared.

*Do not worry; to them this is but the briefest of moments.* He stood in front of her then, in his true form, his ebony wings arching from his back and his horns on his head.

Schuyler looked at the band on her finger and saw that it was a ring of Black Fire.

*Do you know the history of how the angels were made?*

She shook her head.

*When the Almighty created the world, he made the First Born. The Angels of the Light: Michael, Gabrielle, and their brethren were fashioned from the gossamer stars of the heavens. The Angels of the Underworld were cast from the Dark Matter that holds the*

*Earth. There is no Light without the Dark. I am made of fire and iron, of coal and brimstone.*

*When we were cast out of Paradise, we lost part of our soul forever. As part of our punishment, we were cursed never to learn to love again. Instead, we were bound to a destiny that was set from the beginning. Azrael and I never chose each other; the choice was made for us. We never knew anything else.*

*The ring you hold is part of my soul that your mother helped me recover. It was she who saved us from the Dark and led us back to the Light. As her daughter, you too are an Angel of the Light. The fire does not harm you. I lost this ring during the crisis in Rome. But now it has been returned to me.*

*This ring has been blessed by Gabrielle herself.*

*I have never given this ring, my soul, to anyone. Azrael has never had any part of this.*

*This is the only part of myself that is truly mine, and now it is yours.*

When they stepped away from the glom, Schuyler marveled at the dark ring in her hand. It looked so plain and ordinary, and yet behind it was a secret history of war and blood and love and loss and forgiveness and friendship.

"I will never take it off," she promised. "And I have a ring as well."

This time, her hands were as steady as a surgeon's as she slipped the ring on his finger. It was a plain gold ring. Inscribed with her parents' wedding date. When she left New York, she had managed to bring a few prized possessions with her.

*This was my father's ring*, she sent. *It has a protection in it that my mother bestowed on him when they bonded. I want you to have it.*

They took each other's hands, and in front of a chapel filled with their friends, they said the words that bound them to each other, words that could not be unmade.

"I give myself to you and accept you as my own," Jack declared, his voice trembling a little. There were tears in his eyes.

"I give myself to you and accept you as my own," Schuyler echoed. She felt calm and serene and looked at him with so much love.

It was done.

They were bonded.

When she looked at Jack again, his emerald eyes were dancing. He radiated joy and happiness and pride. She swelled with love. Against everything, they were together. Against everything, she was his and he was hers.

Did she feel different? Somehow she had imagined an invisible bond forming between them, a physical sensation tying them to each other. Yet she felt the same. Only better. Only more complete. More at peace.

The small room burst into cheering and applause.

When they walked out of the church to the cheerful strains of Mendelssohn's "Wedding March," their friends greeted them with bright sparklers that shone against the darkness and called their names to the skies.

Jack tightened his grip on her hand, and Schuyler squeezed back twice. It was their secret code. It meant *I love you*.

Tomorrow Jack would leave her. Tomorrow he would return to New York and she would head for Alexandria.

But tonight, they would dance.

## *Acknowledgments*

Thank you from the bottom of my heart to my family. Mike and Mattie. Mom. Aina, Steve, Nicholas, and Josey. Chit and Christina. Mom and Dad J and all the other J's. Miss you, Pop. Thank you to my lovely editors, Christian Trimmer and Stephanie Lurie, and everyone at Hyperion. Thank you to my wonderful agent, Richard Abate. Thank you to all of you who have been with the Blue Bloods for so long. *Arrivederci* for now. See you again soon.

If you haven't read the latest Blue Bloods novel,
turn the page for an enthralling preview from

# Misguided Angel

## From the Personal Journal
## of Lawrence Van Alen

There were seven of us at the inception of the order. A conclave was called to address the growing threat posed by the Paths of the Dead. Along with myself, present at the gathering were the Emperor's cousin Gemellus, a weakling; Octilla and Halcyon from the vestal virgins; General Alexandrus, head of the Imperial Army; Pantaelum, a trusted senator; and Onbasius, a healer.

In my prodigious research I have determined that Halcyon was most likely the keeper of the Gate of Promise, the third known Gate of Hell. I have come to the conclusion that this gate is instrumental in uncovering the truth behind the continued existence of our supposedly vanquished enemies. This is the gate we must focus on, the most important one in the lot.

From what I can deduce, Halcyon settled in Florence, and it is my belief that her latest recorded incarnation was as Catherine of Siena, a famous Italian mystic "born" in 1347. However, after Catherine's "death," there is no other record of a prominent female presence in the city. It appears she had no heirs to her name, and her line simply disappears after the end of Giovanni de Medici's rule in 1429.

From the fifteenth century onward, the city becomes the center of the growing power of the Petruvian Order, founded by the ambitious priest Father Benedictus Linardi. The Petruvian school and monastery are currently under the leadership of one Father Roberto Baldessarre. I have written to Father Baldessarre and leave for Florence tomorrow.

# A Chase

*The sound of footsteps on cobblestone echoed throughout the empty streets of the city. Tomasia kept the pace, her kidskin slippers hardly making a sound, while behind her came the slap of Andreas's heavy boots and Giovanni's lighter step. They ran in a single file, a tight unit, used to this kind of discipline, used to blending in with the dark. When they arrived at the middle of the square, they separated.*

*Tomi flew up the nearest cornerstone and perched on a cornice looking over the broad panorama of the city: the half-built dome of the Basilica to the Ponte Vecchio and beyond the river. She sensed the creature was near and prepared to strike. Their target still did not know he was being followed, and her blow would be immediate and invisible, every trace of the Silver Blood eradicated and extinguished—almost as if the beast—disguised as a palace guard—never existed. Even the creature's last gasp must be silent. Tomasia kept her position, waiting for the creature to come to her, to walk into the trap they had laid.*

She heard Dre grunting, a bit out of breath, and then next to him, Gio, his sword already unsheathed, as they followed the vampire into the alley.

This was her chance. She flew down from her hiding place, holding her dagger with her teeth.

But when she landed, the creature was nowhere to be found.

"Where—?" she asked, but Gio put a finger to his mouth and motioned to the alleyway.

Tomi raised her eyebrows. This was unusual. The Silver Blood had stopped to converse with a hooded stranger. Strange: the Croatan despised the Red Bloods and avoided them unless they were torturing them for sport.

"Should we?" she asked, moving toward the alley.

"Wait," Andreas ordered. He was nineteen, tall and broad, with sculpted muscles and a ferocious brow—handsome and ruthless. He was their leader, and had always been.

Next to him, Gio looked elfin, almost fey, with a beauty that could not be denied or hidden under his scraggly beard and long, unkempt hair. He kept his hand on his weapon, tense and ready to spring.

Tomi did the same, and caressed the sharp edge of her dagger. It made her feel better to know it was there.

"Let's watch what happens," Dre decided.

# PART THE FIRST

## SCHUYLER VAN ALEN AND THE GATE OF PROMISE

Off the Italian Coast

The Present

## ONE

*The Cinque Terre*

chuyler Van Alen walked as quickly as she could up the polished brass spiral stairs leading to the upper deck. Jack Force was standing at the edge of the bow when she caught his eye. She nodded to him, shielding her eyes from the hot Mediterranean sun. *It's done.*

*Good,* he sent, and went back to setting the anchor. He was sunburned and shaggy, his skin a deep nut brown, his hair the color of flax. Her own dark hair was wild and unkempt from a month of salty sea air. She wore an old shirt of Jack's that had once been white and pristine and was now gray and ragged at the hems. They both displayed that laconic, relaxed air affected by those on perpetual vacation: a lazy, weathered aimlessness that belied their true desperation. A month was long enough. They had to act now. They had to act today.

The muscles on Jack's arms tensed as he tugged on the rope to see if the anchor had found purchase on the ocean floor. No luck. The anchor heaved, so he released the line a few more feet. He raised a finger over his right shoulder, signaling to Schuyler to reverse the port engine. He let the rope go a little farther and tugged at it again, the stout white braids of the anchor line chafing his palm as he pulled it toward him.

From her summers sailing on Nantucket, Schuyler knew that an ordinary man would have used a motor winch to set the seven-hundred-pound anchor, but of course Jack was far from ordinary. He pulled harder—using almost all of his strength, and all eight tons of the Countess's yacht seemed to flex for a moment. This time the anchor held, wedged into the rocky bottom. Jack relaxed and dropped the rope, and Schuyler moved from the helm to help him twine it around the base of the winch. In the past month they'd each found quiet solace in these small tasks. It gave them something to do while they plotted their escape.

For while Isabelle of Orleans had welcomed them to the safety of her home, Jack remembered that once upon a time, in another lifetime, Isabelle had been Lucifer's beloved, Drusilla, sister-wife to the emperor Caligula. True, the Countess had been more than generous toward them: she had blessed them with every comfort—the boat, in particular, was fully staffed and bountifully stocked. Yet it was becoming clearer each day that the Countess's offer of protection was morphing from asylum to confinement. It was already November and they were virtual prisoners in her care, as they were never left alone, nor were they allowed to leave. Schuyler and Jack were as far from finding the Gate of Promise as they had been when they'd left New York.

The Countess had given them everything except what they needed most: freedom. Schuyler did not believe that Isabelle, who had been a great friend to Lawrence and Cordelia, and was one of the most respected vampire dowagers of European society, was a Silver Blood traitor. But of course, given the recent events, anything seemed possible. In any event, if the Countess was planning on keeping them prisoner for perpetuity, they couldn't afford to wait and find out.

Schuyler glanced shyly at Jack. They had been

together a month now, but even though they were finally an official couple, everything felt so new—his touch, his voice, his companionship, the easy feel of his arm around her shoulder. She stood beside him against the rail, and he looped his arm around her neck, pulling her closer so he could plant a quick kiss on the top of her head. She liked those kisses the most, found a deep contentment at the confident way he held her. They belonged to each other now.

Maybe this was what Allegra had meant, Schuyler thought, when she had told her to come home and stop fighting, stop fleeing from finding her own happiness. Maybe this was what her mother wanted her to understand.

Jack lowered his arm from her shoulder, and she followed his gaze to the small rowboat "the boys" were lowering from the stern onto the choppy water below. They were a jolly duo, two Italians, Drago and Iggy (short for Ignazio), Venators in service to the Countess and, for all intents and purposes, Jack and Schuyler's jailers. But Schuyler had come to like them almost as friends, and the thought of what she and Jack were about to do set her nerves on edge. She hoped the Venators would be spared from harm, but she and Jack would do what they had to. She marveled at his calm demeanor; she herself could barely keep still, bouncing up and down on the balls of her feet in anticipation.

She followed Jack to the edge of the platform. Iggy had tethered the little boat to the yacht, and Drago reached forward to help Schuyler step down. But Jack slipped ahead and brushed Drago aside so he could offer Schuyler his palm instead, ever the gentleman. She held his hand as she climbed over the rail and into the boat. Drago shrugged and steadied the boat as Iggy brought the last of the provisions onto the bow—several picnic baskets and backpacks filled with blankets and water. Schuyler patted her bag, confirming that the Repository files with Lawrence's notes were in their usual place.

Schuyler turned to look closely upon the rugged Italian coast for the first time. Ever since they had learned of Iggy's affinity for the Cinque Terre, they had been advocating for this little day trip. The Cinque Terre was a strip of the Italian Riviera populated by a series of five medieval towns. Iggy, with his broad face and fat belly, spoke longingly of running along the paths along the cliff edge before coming home to outdoor dinners overlooking sunsets above the bay.

She had never been to this part of Italy and did not know too much about it—but she understood how they could use Iggy's affection for his hometown to their advantage. He had not been able to resist their suggestion to visit, and allowed them a day off of their floating prison. It was the perfect spot for what they had planned, as trails ended in ancient stairs that stretched upward for hundreds of feet. The paths would be abandoned this time of year—tourist season was over, as fall brought cold weather to the popular resort towns. The mountain trails would lead them far from the ship.

"You are going to love this place, Jack," Iggy said, rowing vigorously. "You too, *signorina*," he said. The Italians had a difficult time pronouncing *Schuyler*.

Jack grunted, pulling on his oar, and Schuyler tried to affect a festive air. They were supposed to be getting ready for a picnic. Schuyler noticed Jack brooding, staring at the sea, preparing himself for the day ahead, and she swatted his arm playfully. This was supposed to be a long-awaited respite from their time on the ship, a chance to spend a day exploring.

They were supposed to look like a happy couple with not a care in the world, not like two captives about to execute a prison break.

Schuyler felt her mood lift as they pulled into the bay at Vernazza. The view could bring a smile to anyone's face, and even Jack brightened. The rock ledges were spectacular and the houses that clung to them looked as ancient as the stones themselves. They docked the boat, and the foursome hiked up the cliff side toward the trail.

The five towns that formed the Cinque Terre were connected by a series of stony paths, some almost impossible to climb, Iggy explained, as they walked past a succession of tiny stucco homes. The Venator was in a jubilant mood, telling them the history of every house they walked past. "And this one, my aunty Clara sold in 1977 to a nice family from Parma, and this right here was where the most beautiful girl in Italy lived"—Iggy made a kissing noise—"but . . . Red Blood lady you know how they are . . . *picky* . . . Oh and this is where . . ."

Iggy called out to farmers as they walked through the backyards and fields, patting animals as they strolled past their pastures. The trail wound back and forth from grassland to homes to the very edge of the sea cliffs.

Schuyler watched tiny rocks tumble over the side of the hill as they made their way forward. Iggy kept the conversation flowing, while Drago nodded and laughed to himself, as if he had taken the tour one time too many and was merely humoring his friend. The climb was hard work, but Schuyler was glad for the chance to stretch her muscles, and she was certain Jack was too. They had spent too much time on the boat, and while they had been allowed to swim in the ocean, it wasn't the same as a good hike in the open air. In a few hours they had moved from Vernazza to Corniglia and then Manarola. Schuyler noticed that they passed the day without seeing a single car or truck, not a phone line or power cable.

*This is it,* Jack sent. *Over there.*

Schuyler knew it meant he had judged their distance to be nearly halfway between the last two towns. It was time. Schuyler tapped Iggy on the shoulder and gestured toward a craggy outcropping that hung over the cliff side. "Lunch?" she asked, her eyes twinkling.

Iggy smiled. "Of course! In all my exuberance I forgot to let us stop and eat!"

The spot Schuyler had led them to was in a peculiar location. The trail stretched out toward a promontory so that there were cliffs on either side of the narrow path. The two Venators spread one of the countess's spotless white tablecloths over a grassy plateau between the rough stone, and the four of them crammed into the small space. Schuyler tried not to gaze down as she snuggled up as close to the edge as possible.

Jack sat across from her, gazing over her shoulder at the shoreline below. He kept his eyes on the beach as Schuyler helped unpack the basket. She brought out salamis and prosciutto di Parma, finocchiona, mortadella, and air-cured beef. Some of the meat came in long rolls, while others were cut into small disks and wrapped in wax paper. There was a loaf of rosemary cake, along with a brown paper bag full of almond tarts and jam crostata. It was a pity it was all going to go to waste. Drago pulled several plastic containers filled with Italian cheeses—pecorino and fresh burrata wrapped in green asphodel leaves. Schuyler tore off a piece of the burrata and took a bite. It was buttery and milky, equal to the view in splendor.

She caught Jack's eyes briefly. *Get ready*, he sent. She continued to smile and eat, even as her stomach clenched. She turned briefly to see what Jack had seen. A small motorboat had pulled up to the beach below. Who would have known a teenage North African pirate from the Somali coast would prove to be such a reliable contact, Schuyler thought. Even from far above she could see that he had brought them what they had asked for: one of the pirate crew's fastest speedboats, jerry-rigged with a grossly oversized engine.

Iggy popped open a bottle of Prosecco, and the four of them toasted the sun-drenched coastline with friendly smiles. He lifted his hand in a wide gesture as he gazed down at the midday feast. "Shall we begin?"

That was the moment she had been waiting for. Schuyler sprung into action. She leaned back and appeared to lose her balance for a moment, then bent forward and tossed the full contents of her wineglass into Drago's face. The alcohol stung his eyes, and he looked baffled, but before he could react, Iggy slapped him on the back and guffawed heartily, as if Schuyler had made a particularly funny joke.

With Drago momentarily blinded, and Iggy's eyes closed in laughter, Jack moved to strike. He slid a shank out from his shirtsleeve and into his palm, flipped it around and drove the knife deep into Drago's chest, sending the Italian sprawling to the ground, bleeding. Schuyler had helped Jack make the blade from one of the deck boards. He had hollowed out the back of a loose stair tread and carved it against a stone she'd found from a dive. The shank was made from ironwood, and it made for a dangerous and deadly little dagger.

Schuyler rushed for the other Venator, but Iggy was gone before she could stand. This they had not counted on. The fat man could *move*. In an instant he had pulled the shank from his friend's chest to use as a weapon of his own and turned toward Schuyler, the laughter having died from his eyes.

"Jack!" she cried as the Venator charged. She suddenly couldn't move. Iggy had hit her with a stasis spell when he'd stolen the blade, which he was now holding above her chest. In a moment it would pierce her heart—but Jack dove between them and took the full brunt of the blow.

Schuyler had to get out of the spell. She wrenched herself forward with every ounce of energy, fighting the invisible web that held her. The sensation was like moving in slow motion through a thick ooze, but she found the spell's weak link and broke through. She screamed as she ran toward Jack's seemingly lifeless body.

Iggy got there first, but as he turned Jack over, he did a double take. Jack was unharmed, alive, and smiling grimly.

He leapt to his feet. "Tsk, tsk, Venator. How could you forget an angel cannot be harmed with a blade of his own making?" Jack rolled up his sleeves as he faced his adversary. "Why don't you make it easy on yourself?" he said mildly. "I suggest you go back and tell the Countess that we are not a pair of trinkets she can keep in a jewelry box. Go now, and we will leave you unharmed."

For a moment it appeared as if the Venator was about to consider the offer, but Schuyler knew he was too old a soul to take such a cowardly route. The Italian removed a nasty-looking curved blade from his pocket and pounced toward Jack, but suddenly stopped in mid-air. He hung there for second with a funny look on his face, part confusion and part defeat.

"Nice move with the stasis," Jack said, turning to Schuyler.

"Anytime." She smiled. She had taken the edges of

the spell that had paralyzed her and hit the Venator with it.

Jack took it from there, and with a powerful gesture, he threw the fat guard off the side of the cliff, sending him crashing to the water below. Schuyler rolled the unconscious Drago to the edge and threw him over as well, to join his friend in the ocean.

"You got the tank?" Jack asked as they scrambled down the face of the cliff to the pirate boat waiting for them below.

"Of course." She nodded. They had planned their escape well: Jack had driven the yacht's anchor impossibly deep into the rocky ocean bottom, while Schuyler had emptied the yacht's fuel supply. The night before they had sabotaged the boat's sails and the radio.

They ran across the beach toward the pirate boat, where their new friend Ghedi was waiting for them. Schuyler had befriended him during one of their supervised trips to the Saint-Tropez market, where the former member of the self-styled "Somali Marines" was helping unload a pallet of fresh fish upon the dock. Ghedi missed his days of adventure and jumped at the chance to help the two trapped Americans.

"All yours, bossing." Ghedi smiled, showing a row of gleaming white teeth. He was lithe and quick, with a merry, handsome face and skin the color of burnished cocoa. He jumped off the starboard. He would catch a ride back to the market on the ferry.

"Thanks, man," Jack said, taking the wheel. "Check your accounts tomorrow."

The Somali grinned more widely, and Schuyler knew the fun of stealing the boat was almost payment enough.

The massive engine roared to life as they sped away from the shore. Schuyler glanced to where the two Venators were floating lifelessly in the water. She comforted herself with the knowledge that both would survive. They were ancient creatures and no cliff-side fall could truly harm them; only their egos would be bruised. Still, they wouldn't be able to recover for a while, and by then she and Jack would be well on their way.

She exhaled. Finally. On to Florence, to begin the search for the keepers and secure the gate before the Silver Bloods found it. They were back on track.

"All right?" Jack asked, guiding the ship with expert ease through the stormy waves. He reached for her hand and squeezed it tightly.

She held it against her cheek, loving the feel of his

rough calluses against her skin. They had done it. They were together. Safe. Free. Then she froze. "Jack, behind us."

"I know. I hear the engines," he said, without even bothering to look over his shoulder.

Schuyler stared at the horizon, where three dark shapes had appeared. More Venators, on Jet Skis with a black-and-silver cross insignia emblazoned on the windshields. Their forms grew larger and larger as they drew closer. Apparently Iggy and Drago hadn't been their only jailers.

Escape was going to be harder than they thought.

## THREE

*Into the Deep*

The first drops of rain fell like gentle kisses on her cheek, and Schuyler hoped it would be nothing but a mild shower. But a glance at the ever-darkening sky told her otherwise. The calm blue horizon was now a palette of gray, red, and black; the clouds swirled together to form a heavy, solid mass. The rain, which had begun like a quiet afterthought, suddenly drummed against the deck in a rising staccato. The thunder cracked, a deep rumbling boom that made her jump.

Of course it had to rain. Just to make everything more complicated. Schuyler reached behind Jack and holstered a short bow they had asked Ghedi to procure and stow in the smuggler's locker, a hidden compartment located in the bilge.

During their month at sea they had passed the

time by preparing for this escape. After hours, Jack had schooled Schuyler in the fine points of Venator craft (subterfuge, ammunition), and with Iggy's and Drago's approval, had taught Schuyler a rudimentary course in archery. With her steady hand and eye, she had proven an even better shot than Jack. She removed several ironwood arrows from her pack, more handmade weapons fashioned during their captivity. Schuyler holstered one against the bow and took position.

Their pursuers were still a long way behind for now. She could see them clearly even through the wind and fog. She bent her knees slightly and willed herself to be a statue in the moving sea, raising the bow and drawing the arrow as far back as she could. When she was sure she had her mark, she let it fly. But the Jet Ski expertly dodged away.

Unperturbed, she reloaded the bow. This time when she drew the arrow it lodged into a Venator's knee. The Jet Ski swerved uncontrollably in the water, and Schuyler felt triumphant until the Venator righted up again, unfazed by his gaping wound.

Meanwhile, Jack kept his eyes straight ahead, a steady hand on the throttle. He was giving the engine everything it had, and it was burning up too fast and too hot—throwing off a shower of sparks and making a horrid sputtering noise.

Schuyler looked behind them again. Their pirate boat was doing the best it could, but it wouldn't be long before they were overtaken. The Venators were much closer now, no more than fifty feet away. It rained even harder, and she and Jack were both soaked to the bone, as the wind whipped up the waves and the boat rose and fell in a treacherous, roller-coaster fashion.

She planted her feet, hoping to get more leverage, as columns of water surged onto the deck. She only had two arrows left; she had to make them count. She armed up and poised to strike, just in time to see something fiery and blazing aimed right at her.

"Schuyler!" Jack yelled, pulling her down just as something exploded in the air where she had been standing. Good God, the Venators were fast—she hadn't even seen her assailant take aim and fire.

Jack kept one hand on the steering wheel, the other hand he kept protectively at her back. "Hellfire," he muttered as another explosion barely missed the starboard and shook the ship. The missiles were outfitted with the deadliest weapon in the Venators' arsenal: the Black Fire of Hell, the only thing on earth that could end the immortal blood running in their veins.

"But why would they want us dead?" Schuyler asked, above the roar of the storm as she held the bow to her side. Surely the Countess did not wish them that much ill will. Did she hate them that much?

"We're collateral damage now," Jack said. "She was only keeping us alive while it was convenient to her. But now that we've escaped, her ego can't take it. She'll kill us just to make a point. That no one defies the Countess."

The boat bounced across the swelling waves, each time landing with a hard jolt, a rickety crunch of bolt and nail against wood and water. The engine was shot. It felt as if it was only by their sheer will that the makeshift speedboat held together.

Another blast rocked the helm of the ship, closer this time. The next one would sink them. Schuyler leapt from her hiding place, and in quick inhuman succession, pulled off the last two shafts. This time her arrows pierced the gas tank of the nearest Jet Ski, which exploded upon impact.

They didn't have time to celebrate, as another missile sailed over the bow, and Jack turned the wheel sharply to the right only to come directly upon a ten-foot-tall wave that swallowed the ship whole.

The pirate boat burst through to the other side, miraculously still intact.

Schuyler looked over her shoulder. Two Venators left, they were so close she could see the outline of their goggles and the silver stitching on their leather gloves. The Venators' faces were impassive. They didn't care if she and Jack lived or died, if they were innocent or guilty. They only took orders, and their orders were to shoot to kill.

A crashing wave took them precariously off balance, the ship tilting forward until it was almost vertical, then slammed back hard on the opposite end. Any moment now they were bound to capsize. They were out of arrows. They were out of options.

*We'll have to ditch the ship. We'll go faster if we swim*, Schuyler sent. It was the same thing Jack was thinking, she knew. It was just hard for him to say it. Because swimming meant being separated from each other. *Don't worry. I am strong. As are you.* She exchanged a wry smile with her love.

Jack gripped the steering wheel, his jaw clenched. *You're sure?*

*Meet me in Genoa*, she told him. The nearest coastal town from their current location. Thirty miles to the north.

He nodded, and a picture appeared in her mind, to show he knew it as well. A crowded port city ringed by mountains, colorful boats of every stripe bobbing in the harbor. From there they could hike through the rugged terrain to Florence.

*Swim out as far as you can. I'll aim the ship at the remaining Jet Skis*, Jack sent. He held her gaze for a moment.

Schuyler nodded.

*On my count.*

I can do this, Schuyler thought. I know I will see Jack again. I believe it.

There wasn't any time for a last kiss, or a last word of any sort. She felt Jack's countdown more than heard it— her body executing the commands before her brain could register them. By "three" she was already diving off the edge, already plowing down into the deep, dark water, already kicking her legs against the tide, already measuring her breath. As a vampire she could swim underwater for longer stretches than her human counterparts—but she would have to be careful not to waste energy.

Above the surface she heard a sickening crash as the pirate ship slammed into their enemies. The darkness of the sea was absolute, but after a while Schuyler's eyes adjusted. She pushed her hands against the water, churning, churning, muscles pushing and aching against the heavy water. She watched the bubbles rise to the surface. She could go five minutes without air, and she had to make good use of it. At last her lungs screamed for oxygen, and she began to kick up toward the surface—she had no desire now except to breathe—so close—so close—yes—one more kick and she would break through—yes. . . .

A cold, bony hand grasped her ankle, keeping her down, pulling her back into the deep.

Schuyler squirmed and kicked. She twisted so that she could see who was holding her. Below, a female Venator seemed to float effortlessly in the dark water. Her attacker assessed her coolly and continued to pull. *You are under the protection of the Countess. To deny this protection is an act against the Coven. Submit or be destroyed.*

The hand gripped her ankle in a solid lock. Schuyler could feel herself weakening—she would pass out soon if she didn't get air. Her lungs were about to burst. She was dizzy and starting to panic. Stop it, she told herself. She had to be calm.

The glom. Use the glom. *RELEASE ME*, she demanded, sending a compulsion so strong she could feel the words taking physical form, each letter an attack upon the Venator's cerebellum. The hand on her ankle shook slightly, and that was all Schuyler needed.

She burst away just as the Venator sent a compulsion of her own. Schuyler ducked and sent it back tenfold.

*SINK!*

The compulsion was a punch to the stomach, and the Venator flew backward into the deep, as if propelled downward by a sinking cannonball tied to her ankle. It would take her to the very bottom of the ocean, hopefully giving Schuyler enough time to get away.

She scrambled to get above the waves, finally breaking through to the surface, gasping for air. The rain, cold as a dead man's fingers, lashed her cheeks. She chanced a look back.

Their little motorboat was on fire. Burning, with sparks of black flames shooting up toward the heavens.

Jack made it out, she told herself. Of course he did. He had to.

A few feet away, Schuyler could see another Jet Ski circling the fiery carcass. But why hadn't that Venator gone after Jack, Schuyler wondered. Unless . . . unless he was already . . .

She couldn't finish the thought.

She wouldn't.

She pushed her head underneath the waves. The Genoa port. She began to swim.

## FOUR

## *Driftwood*

*E*verything around Schuyler was black, as dark above as below. If she swam below the ocean's surface she found she could make better time, and took to swimming deep underwater for longer and longer periods. Schuyler pushed against the current, buffeted by the waves; she felt as insignificant as flotsam, just another piece of ocean rubbish lost in the tide. She had to fight the desire to give in, to stop swimming, to close her eyes and rest and drown.

The storm broke for a moment, and Schuyler, bobbing up, could see the city rising from the water, its cheerful pastel buildings only a few hundred feet away. The midday sun was shining brightly on the pretty waterfront cafés. It was past high season, and the weather was brisk, so the outdoor tables were empty.

Schuyler tread water furiously to keep her head above the waves. God, she was tired. She was so close, but she didn't know if she could make it.

That was the problem with the *Velox*, Lawrence had warned her. You begin to believe in your superhuman capabilities, but the *Velox* demands rest, and it will have it whether you liked it or not. He had warned her of vampires who had pushed themselves to the limit, only to collapse at a crucial juncture and be overtaken by the Silver Bloods.

She had no more energy left; she couldn't propel herself the last few tantalizing feet to reach her goal.

She felt as limp as plankton. All the strength had drained from her body. She had covered about twenty-five miles in half an hour, but it wasn't enough to get her onto that nearby beach. She spit out some salt water and pushed her bangs out of her eyes, dog-paddling listlessly. Her muscles were torn, spent. She couldn't do one more stroke. . . .

An idea came to her. . . . She couldn't push forward anymore, but she could float. . . . She could just lie down, really, and let the waves do the rest. The thought of backstroking the rest of the way struck her as incredibly ironic after the intensity of her escape. Well, she could float or she could drown. Just as she'd hoped, the slow steady movement required only the amount of energy that she could provide.

A few minutes after setting off on a leisurely pace, she felt the water around her vibrate, and she heard the distinctive motor of a Jet Ski. For a moment she was seized with fear; she kicked upright, looking all around, and then she saw it. Approaching quickly was a familiar vehicle branded with the dreaded black-and-silver cross, but that was no Venator at the helm.

Schuyler bounced up and down on the waves. "GHEDI! GHEDI!" She had no idea how the pirate had come to be on the Jet Ski, but right then she didn't care. All she knew was she had to get his attention before he got too far away.

He couldn't hear her, and the Jet Ski was getting farther and farther away.

*GHEDI. TURN BACK. I COMMAND YOU.*

The Jet Ski swung around, and in a moment, had roared up next to her. "*Signorina!* There you are!" he said, his bright smile splitting his face.

She pulled herself up next to him, thankful to be out of the water at last. "What are you doing here? Where's Jack?"

Ghedi shook his head. After he had bid them

good-bye at the Cinque Terre, he had seen the Venators chase after them. He'd tried to radio them a warning, but the storm had taken out the satellite signals. He'd borrowed a motorboat, and had come upon the wreckage of the pirate ship ("Black, black smoke. Bad.") There had been no sign of Jack, and he'd taken an empty Jet Ski that was most likely left behind by the Venator who had chased Schuyler and who was probably still struggling to swim to the surface.

If Ghedi was here with this Jet Ski, then where was the other Jet Ski with the other Venator, Schuyler wondered. And where was Jack?

* * *

They circled the shoreline for several hours. It would be evening soon. Jack should be here by now, Schuyler thought. It would take a vampire of his speed only minutes to make it. She had managed, and he was by far a stronger swimmer. Schuyler dropped Ghedi off at the harbor, and she continued on the Jet Ski alone, as her new friend was showing signs of fatigue from their search. It wasn't fair to ask him to accompany her on what was looking more and more like a hopeless endeavor.

The sun slipped below the horizon, and the lights

of the city looked festive against the purple sky. Music wafted from the restaurants and cafés by the docks. It was getting colder, and the wind told her the storm would pick up again soon; this was just a momentary calm.

She was going to run out of gas soon, but she made one last round. The night before, she and Jack had made a promise to each other. Whatever happened today, they had agreed they would not wait for the other if they were separated. The journey must continue, regardless of who kept on the path. Whoever remained would carry on Lawrence's legacy.

Okay, Jack, she thought. This is it. You'd better show up or I'm leaving.

She didn't want to think of what it meant, leaving him. She was terrified of being alone, now that she knew what being with Jack was like. He would want her to continue, though. He would want her to leave him, to go ahead without him. She had already wasted enough time.

She would ask Ghedi to help her get to Florence, where Lawrence believed the Gate of Promise was located; she would hike through the mountains as they'd planned. There would be no trains, no little *pensiones*, no rental cars, nothing that would leave a trail. Jack would be able to meet up with her later . . . maybe. . . .

Schuyler tried not to think about it too much. She felt numb from the cold and from what she would have to do. The enormity of her task felt overwhelming. How could she go on alone without knowing what had happened to him, without knowing if he was dead or alive?

Finally she saw it—it looked like driftwood but something about it caught her eye. Anxiously, she came up on it and saw that it was indeed just a piece of driftwood. But clinging to the center of it was a white hand, while the rest of the body was submerged underwater. Schuyler pulled up next to it; she recognized those long, thin fingers, and her heart beat against her chest, the cold creeping through her entire body. Fear. Abject fear.

Jack can't die. He can't die, but he can be harmed. He was immortal, but if it was too late to revive his physical shell, she would have to keep his blood for the next cycle. By the time he was reborn she would be at the end of hers. Who knew if he would love her then? If he would even remember her? In any event, where would she even take his blood? They were fugitives from the vampire community.

She leaned down and grasped his hand, pulling it

gently from the branch. The hand was practically frozen in place, but it returned her grasp and squeezed. He was alive. With all her strength she pulled Jack out of the water in one quick motion and positioned him behind her on the Jet Ski.

He fell against her, his body as cold as an iceberg, and she could feel the weight of his exhaustion against her back. He was barely able to keep his arms around her waist as she pushed off into the darkness.

If she had been just a minute later, who knows what would have become of him. . . . Who knew what would have happened. . . . Who knew what . . .

*Stop your doubting, my love. I knew you would find me.*

Schuyler maneuvered the Jet Ski between two fishing boats and harnessed her craft next to the one that smelled marginally better than the other. The boats were empty, as fishing season was over. The owners would not return until next year. She helped Jack onto the deck of the boat and into its small cabin, which held a ratty couch. How ironic that they had started their day planning to escape from a boat, only to end up in another one.

She helped Jack out of his wet clothes, stripping him

of his shirt, pants, socks, and shoes, and covered him with one of the thin ragged bath towels she'd found in the hold. "Sorry. I know it's not great, but it's all we got."

She rummaged around for supplies, finding a small kerosene lamp in the galley kitchen. She lit the lamp, wishing it would give out more light, or at least more heat. Inside, the boat was almost as cold as it was outside.

"Are you comfortable?" she asked.

He nodded, still unable to speak, either in words or in her mind.

She turned her back and peeled off her own wet things, feeling shy around him, and wrapped herself in a towel as well. The nautical shower was working, probably left with a few gallons of water from its last trip, and she was glad for the opportunity to wash after such a long day. She was also thankful the boat contained a few dry clothes for them to change into: sailor shirts, swim shorts. They would have to do.

After she showered and dressed, Schuyler then helped Jack walk down the few steps into the small bathroom, closing the door behind him.

Thunder rumbled in the distance. It would rain again

soon. The wind howled, lashing against the portholes. Schuyler made sure the latch on the cabin door was secure.

When Jack limped out of the shower, Schuyler was glad to see that he looked a little better. The color had returned to his cheeks. He picked up a blanket from the couch and threw it over his shoulders. "Come here," he whispered, opening his arms so that she could huddle against him, her back against his chest. She could feel his body begin to thaw, and she pulled his arms around her tightly, massaging his hands until they were warm again.

In a soft voice, Jack told her what had happened to him. He had stayed a beat longer on the boat to give Schuyler a head start, and had guided it straight at the Jet Skis. But the Venators had taken that as an opportunity to jump on board, and he had fought them off. One of them had gotten away—the woman who had come after Schuyler. The other one had been a fight to the death.

"What do you mean?" Schuyler asked.

"He had a black sword with him," Jack said slowly, raising a hand to the fire and making the flame leap. "I had to use it. It was him or me." He looked so anguished, Schuyler put a protective hand on his shoulder. Jack bowed his head. "Tabris. I knew him. He was a friend of mine. A long time ago."

Jack had called the Venator by his angel name. Schuyler sucked in her breath. She felt guilty for everything—all this killing—it was all her fault. She had been the one who convinced Jack they should seek refuge with the Countess. She was the one who had brought them to Europe. This quest was her legacy, not his—her responsibility she'd latched on his shoulders. She was the one who had planned their escape—no one was supposed to be hurt. She hadn't realized that the Countess would take it so far—the black sword—dear God. If Jack had not bested the Venator, then he would be the one whose immortal life was finished.

He drew her closer to him and whispered fiercely in her ear. "It had to be done. I gave him a choice. He chose death. Death will come to all, sooner or later." Jack pressed his head against hers, and she could feel the veins throbbing below his skin.

Death will come to all? Jack of all people should know that wasn't true. The Blue Bloods had survived for centuries. Schuyler wondered if he was thinking of Mimi—Azrael—just then. *Death will come to all.* Would it come to Jack? Would Mimi exercise her right to a burning and extinguish Jack's spirit forever?

Schuyler wasn't as concerned about her own mortality as she was of his. If he died, there would be no life for her. Please, God, no. Not yet. Give us this time still. This small sliver of time that we have together, let it last as long as it could.

## FIVE

## *Breaking Bread*

*S*chuyler had fallen asleep in Jack's arms, but she woke up, blinking her eyes, when she heard a rustling noise. The fire in the lamp was still flickering, but the rain had stopped. The only sound was the lapping of waves against the hull. Jack placed a finger to his lips. *Quiet. Someone's here.*

"*Signorina?*" A dark figure hovered by the doorway.

Before Schuyler could answer, Jack had sprung from his seat and held Ghedi by the throat.

"Jack! Wait, what are you doing? It's Ghedi—he helped me! He was the one who got me out of the water, Jack! Let him go!"

Ghedi's dark face had turned several shades of gray. He was holding a basket in his hands, which was now shaking slightly.

"Bossing . . ." he protested. "I bring food. Bread. Dinner."

"You serve us well, human," Jack said coldly. "Maybe too well. Tell us, who do you truly serve?"

Schuyler felt indignation burn her cheeks. "Jack, please! You're being ridiculous!"

"Only if he tells me who he really is and who he's working for. A Somali pirate wouldn't give a rat's ass about two American kids, especially once he was paid. Why did you follow us? Are you a servant of the Countess?"

Ghedi shook his head, and looked them straight in the eye. "Have no fear, my friends, for I am a friend of the professor."

Schuyler was surprised to hear the Somali speaking perfect English, and no longer with the African intonations he'd affected before.

"The professor?" Jack asked, relaxing his grip slightly.

"Professor Lawrence Van Alen, of course."

"You knew my grandfather?" Schuyler asked. "Why didn't you mention it earlier? At the market?"

Ghedi did not reply. Instead, he reached into the basket and brought out sacks of flour, salt, and a small jar of sardines. "First we must eat. I know you do not need it for sustenance, but please, for the sake of companionship, let us share a meal before we discuss."

"Hold on," Jack said. "You speak the names of our friends, yet how do we know you are truly a friend to us? Lawrence Van Alen had as many enemies as allies."

"All you say is true. Yet there is nothing I can show or say that will prove I am who I say I am. You will have to decide for yourself whether I am telling the truth. I have no mark, no papers, nothing that may attest to my story. You have only my word. You must trust your own judgment."

Jack looked at Schuyler. *What do you think?*

*I don't know. You're right to be cautious. But I feel in my heart he is a friend. But that is all I have. A feeling.*

*Instincts are all we have in the end. Instincts and luck,* Jack sent.

Jack said, "We will trust you tonight, Ghedi. You're right, you must eat, as must she. Please . . ." He released his hold and motioned to the fire.

Ghedi whistled while he pounded out the injera dough into small circles in the small galley kitchen. He found a metal skillet and fired up one of the gas burners. With the other, he grilled a few sardines on an open flame.

In a few minutes, the bread began to rise, puffing with small indentations. The fish began to smoke. When it was ready, Ghedi prepared three plates.

The bread was a bit sour and spongy, but Schuyler thought it was the best thing she had ever eaten. She didn't even realize until she smelled the fresh, delicious aroma filling the room that she was hungry. Starving even. The fish was excellent, and along with a few fresh tomatoes Ghedi had unearthed, it made a satisfying meal. Jack had a piece or two, to be polite. But Schuyler and Ghedi ate as if it was their last meal.

So it wasn't a coincidence, then, their meeting Ghedi at the market, Schuyler thought, apprising their new companion as she dipped a piece of bread into the small pool of ghee on her plate. When she thought about it a little more, she remembered that it was the pirate who had approached them. And now, on further recollection, it seemed that he was waiting for them. He had practically ambushed them when they had walked past his stall, asking if there was any way he could be of service. He had been quite persuasive, and somehow Schuyler had managed to communicate the specifics of their confinement, and they had finally agreed to trust him with getting them a motorboat.

But who *was* Ghedi after all? How did he know Lawrence?

"I know you have many questions," the Somali said. "But it is late. And we must all rest. Tomorrow, I will return and tell you what I know."